A Body in My Office

THE CHARLES BENTLEY MYSTERIES, Volume 1

Glen Ebisch

Published by Glen Ebisch, 2021.

A BODY IN MY OFFICE

First edition. July 23, 2021.

Written by Glen Ebisch.

Table of Contents

Chapter One

"This is the last day of the rest of your life," Yuri said with a benign smile.

Charles Bentley glanced at him in some alarm then comprehension dawned.

"You mean this is the first day of the rest of my life."

Yuri, looking stricken, fumbled a small spiral notebook out of his shirt pocket and began to write a note to himself. Although Yuri was from somewhere in the former Soviet bloc, his field of specialization was twentieth century English literature, and if the rumors that Charles had heard around the College were true, he was amazingly capable at explaining the most thorny passages of James Joyce so that even freshmen could understand and appreciate them. All that being said, however, he had terrible difficulties with American colloquialisms, and every time he got one wrong he would carefully correct himself in his notebook. Charles imagined that his desk must be filled with piles of them. But none of this self-criticism seemed to help, and he continued to make the same old errors and add new ones.

"Why would you say that?" Charles asked. "That phrase implies that somehow today is a major turning point for me."

Yuri answered with another smile. As far as Charles knew, he and Yuri were waiting outside the Dean's office to meet with him to discuss the course offerings in American literature for the next five years. Yuri's words, now properly interpreted, suggested the something else was afoot. Treachery and deceit were not unknown at Opal College, a highly respected four-year liberal arts college in Opalsville, Massachusetts, with a campus sprawling across several hillsides in the Berkshires of Massachusetts. Charles suspected they had not been unknown even in the mid-eighteenth century when Rickford Opal, a prosperous fur trader and politician, founded the institution. The methods may have been polished and refined over time, but the consequences could still be devastating to the victim.

The door to the Dean's office opened and Walter Carruthers stepped out into the anteroom. He looked at the two men and gave an affable chuckle, which to Charles' mind was only a short step away from the sadistic cackle Robespierre would have made at the sweet sound of the tumbrel passing by. Carruthers' pudgy hand, attached to a similar body, motioned for them to come into the office. Charles stumbled slightly on the smooth carpet, which he took as a sign from the universe that this was going to be a bad day.

Carruthers' cavernous office had two walls lined with books, most on sociology, his purported field of study, although he had been an administrator for so long no one could remember the last time he had taught a student. A vanity wall behind his desk was covered with rows of diplomas and certificates. Charles often suspected they went back far enough in time that his election to his high school honor society was probably among them. Yuri and Charles were seated in front of the Dean's desk like two unruly schoolboys about to be reprimanded. Carruthers put his elbows on the desktop, steepled his fingers, and frowned as if he felt either indigestion or an idea coming on.

"As you both know, colleges today, especially on our level, are faced with the problem of maintaining our high standards. One of the ways we do this is by accepting only a miniscule percentage of our applicants. But equally important, we must be able to show parents and the public alike that the very best of scholarship is being done here, and that we are equal, if not superior to, the other schools with which we are competing for the crème de la crème. We must, in short, justify charges for tuition, room and board that equal the mortgage payments on a small mansion."

"We must prove we are the tip of the heap," Yuri said enthusiastically.

Carruthers looked at him in puzzlement.

"That's 'top of the heap,'" Charles said softly. Yuri quickly whipped out his notebook.

"Anyway," Carruthers went on, "in order to do this, we must guarantee that every department has the requisite number of outstanding scholars. Stars—if I may use such a meretricious term with regard to academic accomplishment. And my overview of humanities has revealed that we are somewhat deficient in stars in the area of English literature."

"Oh, I don't know about that. We still have Rawlings in nineteenth century and Mercer is starting to make a name for himself in twentieth century poetry," Charles objected, offering a defense of the department that Yuri should be vigorously seconding instead of scribbling in his damned notebook.

Carruthers shrugged, clearly unimpressed. "And what about in American literature?"

"There's only Andrea Boyd and myself. She's coming along well with five articles in the last four years, and hopefully will have a book out in a couple more years."

"I really meant, what about you?" Carruthers sat back and stared hard at Charles.

"What about me? I think my credentials speak for themselves."

"Perhaps they did at one time, Charles, but what have you produced in the last three years."

Charles sat silently. In the three years since his wife Barbara had died, he hadn't been able to focus on anything other than the bare requirements to teach his courses. Whenever he tried to return to an unfinished article or book chapter, his mind would drift back to what he had been doing with Barbara at the time it had been started, and after several hours had passed, he'd find he hadn't written a thing.

"I'm aware that you wife's sudden death—

"Let's not go down that road," Charles said so sharply that Carruthers blinked.

"Very well, but you have to admit that you have not attended any conferences, given any presentations or had anything published in the past three years."

"I certainly did plenty before that."

"A good scholar cannot rest on his laurels."

"You haven't even written anything recently on that guy Hawk," the traitorous Yuri said. "The fellow you wrote a book about."

"His name is Bird, Robert Montgomery Bird," Charles said. "And my book was considered definitive. I think there is very little more for me to say."

Carruthers paused and spoke carefully. "There is also the matter of your age. I believe you recently turned sixty-five. People age differently. In fact different parts of them age at different rates. Do you think your failure to pursue scholarship is a function of your age? You look vigorous enough physically, but perhaps your mind has simply outstripped other parts of your body in the process of inevitable decline."

Charles felt the heat rise to his face. "It's illegal to force me to retire because of my age. We shouldn't even be having this discussion."

"Perhaps not. And it is certainly not my intention to force you into retirement. However, my plans for the future of the department will necessitate some rearrangement of resources. Instead of teaching your usual courses in American literature, I'm afraid you will be required instead to teach courses in freshmen composition."

Everyone in English considered freshman composition to be the Sahara of courses, where you trudged from dry paper to dry paper making innumerable corrections and meeting frequently and personally with every student to correct the errors of their writing ways. Meetings not anticipated with pleasure by either the giver or receiver.

"Full professors never teach English comp," Charles pointed out.

"That was true in the past. But as an attempt to elevate the importance of writing in the curriculum we are going to try a little experiment and have a senior faculty member take on that responsibility. Because of your obvious writing skills, you have been selected to be the pioneer in that endeavor."

"And who will be teaching my American literature courses?"

"We are bringing over a fellow from England, a real comer in the field of whom I'm sure you've heard: Garrison Underwood."

Charles clenched his teeth at the recollection of the one time over ten years ago that he'd heard Underwood speak at a conference. He must have mentioned a work of fiction somewhere along the way, but his presentation was so filled with jargon and references to higher criticism that Charles had never grasped his point. If that was typical of Underwood's thinking, he'd be a disaster in the classroom.

"Don't you think it's rather ironic hiring a Brit to teach American literature?" Charles asked.

"Garrison says American literature is too important to be left to Americans," Yuri answered.

"Very clever." Charles gave the Dean a grim smile. "So are you saying that either I retire or I will be teaching only freshmen composition for the rest of my career?"

"I have spoken to the provost, and we are willing to be generous. You will receive two years of your salary as a retirement incentive."

Charles took a deep breath and gave some thought to his options. He really didn't want to give up teaching. What would he do with himself all year? Maybe he could agree to teach freshmen composition and call their bluff. If he didn't vacate his position, there might not be the funds to hire Underwood. He'd hate teaching composition, but at least he'd have the satisfaction of foiling the administration's plans. Then Carruthers spoke. It was as if he'd been reading Charles' mind.

"Underwood will be granted an Opal College Endowed Chair, so he won't be exactly taking over your position. And that way we don't need your salary to pay him. It will come from the special endowment fund."

That meant that even if he continued to teach, they could still hire Underwood, and steal away his courses.

"We would, of course, prefer to have your position vacant, so we can further strengthen the English department with a new hire."

Charles glanced over at Yuri, who suddenly pretended to be interested in the weave of the carpet. So that was why you went along with this, Charles thought, English would get an endowed chair and not lose his position. It was a clear case of academic bribery, but what could he do about it.

"Very well," Charles said softly. "You'll have my letter of retirement by the end of the day."

Carruthers sprang to his feet and extended a hand across his desk.

"Don't be so down about this, Charles. It's a great big world out there. I'm sure you'll find things you enjoy doing other than teaching."

Charles remained silent as he perfunctorily shook Carruthers hand.

When they were once again out in the waiting room, Yuri turned to Charles and said, "Remember, it's always darkest just before dawn."

Charles shook his head. "No, it's always darkest just before it goes black."

"I'm sure I've got that saying right," Yuri protested.

"Not this time," Charles replied.

Yuri remained silent for a moment, not certain what to believe.

"I hate to bring this up, but you'll have to clear out your office by the end of today. Garrison Underwood is already in town, and he would like to get settled in."

"So he gets my office and my job?"

"You know we're short of offices in the English building, Charles. I really had no choice."

"There's always a choice, Yuri. There's always a choice," Charles said grimly.

Chapter Two

Charles and Yuri walked into the department office on the fourth floor of the English building. They hadn't spoken during the walk over from the Dean's office. Charles was lost in his own murky thoughts about the future, and feeling far from cordial to Yuri, who had stabbed him in the back. Yuri immediately disappeared into his office, while Charles stopped to pick up his mail.

"Professor Bentley," said Sheila, the student who was replacing the regular secretary while she was out on vacation for a few days.

Charles looked up from his mail. Sheila stood there staring at the ceiling as if trying to remember why she had spoken to him. Charles waited patiently. There seemed to be frequent gaps in Sheila's thought processes. He wondered whether it was due to the after effects of excessive drug use, the extremely early onset of dementia, or just Sheila being Sheila.

"Oh, yes," she said brightly. "I'm supposed to tell you that Professor Underwood is already here, and he is in your office."

"*In* my office. How did he get in without a key?" Charles asked.

"Umm. I guess I gave him one. He said that he was taking over your office, so I thought it would be all right."

He was about to snap back that it damn well wasn't all right, but he controlled himself. He didn't like to get angry with students. Between hormones and being bossed around by their elders, they were rarely responsible for what they did. Instead he nodded, and with his mail in one hand, he left and headed down the hall to his office. The door was closed, but not locked. When he opened it and went inside, he immediately saw that the top of his desk had been cleaned off. A man with his back toward him was busily replacing the pictures on the wall.

"What's going on here?" Charles demanded.

The man turned around. Charles recognized him as Garrison Underwood, but he had changed dramatically since Charles had heard him speak. Then he had been the picture of vigorous early middle age: handsome, trim, and bright eyed. Although what he had said may have been unintelligible to Charles, he presented it with charm and enthusiasm. The man who faced Charles today had coarsened features, a paunchy waist, and blood shot eyes. He looked like a Hogarth painting on what a life of dissipation could lead to.

"I'm preparing my office if it's any of your business," Underwood snapped.

"I'm Charles Bentley, and as far as I know, this is still my office."

Underwood opened his mouth to speak, then apparently thought better of it. He walked across the room and put his hand out to Charles.

"Sorry to seem a bit precipitate, Bentley, but the old order changeth and all that. I'm scheduled to teach a summer course, so I need to hit the ground running."

Reluctantly Charles took his hand. "I'll need the office for today. I have to get my affairs in order."

That makes it sound like I'm dying, Charles thought, not wanting to be melodramatic, but in a way I suppose I am. Ending a career of almost thirty-five years is a kind of small death.

Underwood reached into a box and took out a large trophy. He placed it on the desk.

"I got that for being best batman on my indoor cricket team at Oxford."

He looked at Charles as if expecting him to be impressed by his excellence at a game that Charles found incomprehensible. When he got no answering look of admiration, Underwood went on quickly, "I've already cleaned your stuff out of the desk. It's all over there he said, pointing to a small box on the floor.

Charles walked over and glanced in the box. Right on top was the picture of Barbara that still graced his desk. The glass in the frame had been shattered.

"You broke my picture," Charles said softly.

"Oh, yes, I dropped it. Of course, I'll pay to have the glass replaced."

Ignoring him, Charles walked back to the desk and, with a graceful motion, swept up the heavy cricket trophy in one hand and threw it across the room. It bounced off the wall, taking a chunk out of the plaster.

"You can't . . . " Underwood said, then a glance at Charles' face caused him to take a step back, and an expression of fear replaced his normal look of disdain.

At that moment Charles could see himself with his hands wrapped around Underwood's throat, cheerfully throttling the life out of him. The image was so real that for a second he imagined it was actually happening. He took a deep breath, struggling to regain self-control.

"Be out of here when I get back," he muttered. Turning on his heel, Charles left the room.

Unaware of his surroundings Charles went down the back stairs and out of the building into the parking lot. There he paced back and forth in front of his car until noticing that he still had his mail clutched in one hand. He opened his car door, threw the mail on the seat, and resumed pacing. He was still pacing several minutes later when he saw Greg Wasserman, his next-door neighbor, who taught physics at the College, walking across the lot toward him.

"How are you doing, Charles?" Wasserman asked with a brief nod, clearly anxious to be on his way.

Although Charles had always considered Greg a bit of a cold fish, an opinion reinforced by the man's tall skeletal body which made it seem as though looking into the abstract fundamentals of things had left him not needing physical nourishment, Charles found himself pouring out to Greg all the details of his trying morning. Greg listened, giving little indication of his point of view either way. When Charles was done, he nodded.

"You know what you need to do?"

Charles wondered whether he was going to be advised to sue Opal College or assassinate the Dean.

"What should I do?"

"Run."

"Run?"

"That's right. A half hour of running every day, and you'll find yourself feeling physically and psychologically healthier. You'll have more energy and not be overwhelmed by adversity. And now that you're retired, you'll have plenty of time for exercise."

"I don't know," Charles said, feeling nervous, as he always did, in the presence of an obvious fanatic.

"Any history of heart problems? Any artificial hips or knees?"

15

"No."

"Then how about we try running together for a few days until you get into the swing of it?"

"Well, that's very nice of you—"

"Structure is as essential to a happy retirement as it is to everything else in life and nature. I'll see you tomorrow in front of your house at seven o'clock."

With a nod, Wasserman marched off to his car. Not being an early riser, Charles wondered whether he could even see the road at such an early hour. He pictured himself running, flashlight in hand, trying to dodge potholes and curbs. The picture wasn't a pretty one.

He resumed pacing, trying to work up his rage in anticipation of returning to his office and tossing Underwood out a window.

"Charles?" a woman's voice asked.

He glanced up and saw Andrea Boyd, the other Americanist, staring at him quizzically. A woman, now in her early thirties, when she had arrived at the college six years ago, Barbara and Charles had taken her under their wing, helping her adapt to New England and Opal College. Andrea was originally a west Texas girl with a mind given to clear and direct thinking. The only time Charles has seen her almost go catatonic was when a snake slithered out of the woodpile behind his house while they were gathering wood for the fireplace. She later explained that being bitten by a rattler as a young girl had given her a Texas sized phobia for snakes.

"Is something wrong, Charles?" she asked, coming over to him. Despite being upset, he found himself admiring her slender waist and long legs.

For the second time in ten minutes, he poured out his tale of woe.

"I'd heard rumors about Underwood being brought in, but I didn't know he was going to replace you."

"Yes, apparently I've reached a time in life when I'm easily expendable."

"You could get a lawyer and fight it on the grounds of age discrimination," Andrea suggested with a determined sound in her voice.

"Even if I won, my golden years would be filled with freshmen composition. No, I think it's time to face the inevitable."

"You could go back up there right and have it out with Underwood. Even if he is taking your job, he should wait for a decent interval before taking your office."

Charles glanced up at his office window. "I think I'm going to do just that."

Andrea smiled. "And after that, why don't we try to look at this as a new beginning? How about I take you out to dinner tonight to celebrate?"

Charles shook his head. "I think I'd rather be alone tonight to think and get my bearings."

"Okay, we'll do it sometime in the next few days," she said, pushing back her shoulder length brown hair.

Since Barbara's death, his feelings for Andrea had been confused. When Barbara was alive, the two of them had clearly been substitute parents for Andrea. After all, she and his daughter Amy were almost the same age. Since Barbara's death, however, he had found himself occasionally entertaining more romantic thoughts about Andrea, then immediately dismissing them as foolish. Only multi-millionaires and aging rock stars had girl friends thirty years younger than themselves. Money and fame were the only substitutes for a wrinkle-free body. Yet the hope never entirely disappeared.

Andrea smiled at him. "Maybe this earthquake in your life will bring something good. You might be motivated to begin a new relationship. After all, it has been three years since Barbara's death." She gave him an innocent glance, which indicated to Charles that she wasn't volunteering herself.

He shrugged, not fully trusting himself to speak about life after Barbara.

Andrea touched his arm. "I know it's hard. We'll talk about it some other time."

He nodded and took a deep breath. "I'll call you about that dinner."

"Do that," she said, waving she went over to her car and drove away.

Charles returned to pacing. The way he saw it this situation could be resolved in three ways. He could return to his office, find it empty, write his letter of resignation, and leave with the box of knickknacks from his desk representing thirty-five years of teaching. He could return to his office, find Underwood still there, and beat the man to a pulp. Finally, he could return to his office, find Underwood still there, and apologize for his hostile behavior.

He was surprised to find that all his pacing, rather than stoking his anger, had actually served to dissipate it. If Underwood was there, and did not further provoke him, he knew he would probably apologize and leave. Slowly he walked across the parking lot, and trudged up the back stairs to his office. The door was closed. When he opened it, there was no sign of anyone in the room. He closed the door behind him and went inside.

When he walked around his desk to use the computer, he saw the body on the floor. It was without a doubt Garrison Underwood. He was lying on his back with his head centered in a rapidly growing pool of blood. Charles knew that death was not always easy to ascertain and that Underwood might only be seriously hurt. But the wide-open eyes staring at the ceiling made him not hold out much hope. Next to Underwood's head was the cricket trophy that Charles had thrown across the room. The murder weapon, no doubt covered with my fingerprints, Charles thought. His first panicky impulse was to run. Get away and let someone else be the first to find the body. But then a sort of fatalistic serenity came over him, and he walked from his office up the hall to the English Department office repeating, "Whatever is going to happen will happen."

He took a couple of steps into the department office. Sheila was bent over, staring at the computer keyboard as if attempting to interpret the letters of a foreign script. She finally looked up.

"Can I help you, Professor Bentley?" she asked, smiling.

"Yes. There's a body in my office."

She stared at him blankly, her smile slowly faltering, much as someone would act if she'd just been told a joke but didn't get the punch line. Charles decided that he clearly needed to provide more information.

"A dead body."

"There's a dead body in your office?" Sheila asked. Her lips twitched nervously as if she suddenly didn't want to be in the same room with someone so clearly unhinged.

"Yes. It's the body of Garrison Underwood. It appears as though he's been murdered."

"Professor Underwood. Murdered?"

Charles nodded encouragingly as if she were a slow student about to finally come upon the correct answer. Sheila, however, refused to take the next practical step, so after waiting a moment, Charles threw aside the Socratic method.

"Call the damned police," he ordered.

Chapter Three

"Hello, I'm Lieutenant Joanna Thorndike, chief of detectives."

Charles wondered how many detectives there could be in a town the size of Opalsville that they needed a chief, but didn't think she would appreciate his asking. They were standing in the English Department seminar room, which the police had requisitioned for conducting interviews. A full coffee pot was on the sideboard. A box of powdered doughnuts occupied the center of the table.

"I see you're not afraid to reinforce stereotypes," Charles said. Then quickly wondered with embarrassment if his reference to police and doughnuts would offend her.

It didn't. She smiled. "I like doughnuts enough not to worry about the consequences, except for those to my waistline."

Charles studied her. She was only a couple of inches shorter than his six feet and looked slender and fit for someone he guessed to be in her early fifties.

"Doesn't look as though you need to worry," he said, and then realized that sounded flirtatious. Probably the first thing murderers do is to try to charm the police, he thought nervously.

"Thanks," Thorndike replied amiably, flashing him a brief grin. "Would you like some coffee or a doughnut?"

He shook his head, nervous and not sure he could eat or drink at the same time as he answered questions.

"Why don't we get started then," she said, putting down a notebook in front of her. "First of all what's your name?"

"Charles Bentley. At least that's one of my names."

"You have aliases," she asked with a deadpan expression.

"No. But my full name is Horace Charles Bentley."

"Really, it sounds better with the first and second names switched."

"My mother thought so as well, but my father's name was Horace, and he insisted on it being first. I never use his name, I go by Charles."

Thorndike looked at him as though he might have serious daddy issues. And maybe I do, what of it? Charles thought defiantly. Don't judge until you've walked a mile in my brogues.

"Before we begin, can I ask whether Underwood was killed with his cricket trophy?" Charles said.

"We won't know without further examination of the body and of the trophy. Why do you ask?"

"Because it will have my fingerprints on it from my first visit to the office."

"You handled the trophy?"

"Not exactly, I threw it across the room."

Thorndike gave a small sigh as if to indicate that nothing was ever easy, and asked him to take his story from the top. He gave his rendition of what had occurred, starting with his interview with the Dean, and ending with finding Underwood dead. Thorndike seemed to be surprised when he said that he threw the trophy because of his wife's picture being broken.

"Not because this man was taking your job?"

"Maybe a little," he answered honestly. "But my anger over that is mostly directed at the college administration. After all, Underwood wouldn't be here if they hadn't offered him the position."

"That's very objective of you."

"I try to be."

The Lieutenant glanced over her notes. "To sum up then, you say you had an argument with the victim. Left him alone and alive in your office, then came back approximately a half hour later and found him dead. You have witnesses who can account for your whereabouts during approximately fifteen minutes of that half hour. For the rest of the time, you say you were alone in the parking lot, pacing."

She glanced at him inquiringly, and Charles nodded.

"So you were alone for fifteen minutes, and could have returned to your office during that period of time."

"I suppose I could have killed Underwood then and waited to announce the discovery of his body. Or I could have killed him before I left the office the first time and then returned to discover him. But I didn't. Wasn't there anyone who saw Underwood during that half hour?"

Thorndike shook her head. "Not that we know about so far. My colleague has spoken briefly with the secretary's assistant, Sheila. She had a good view of the main stairway, and she didn't see anyone go past the open doorway. We're going to interview the other people who were in their offices on the fourth floor."

"What about someone using the back stairs? Could anyone see them?"

She shook her head. "If we had found someone who had their eyes on the backstairs who saw no one other than you using them, this interview would be taking place at the police station, and you would have been informed of your rights."

Charles sat back in the chair, his heart beating rapidly.

"Because then you'd think I must have killed him."

She nodded. "Of course that's still that possibility, but we can't be certain."

"Talk to Greg and Andrea, they'll tell you that I wasn't acting like a killer in the parking lot."

"And how does a killer act? Does he froth at the mouth? Curse loudly? Declare that he's glad he killed the bastard? In my experience, that happens very rarely. And pacing back and forth in the parking lot is not exactly normal behavior."

"I'd had a bad morning," Charles said, slumping back in the chair dejectedly, wondering if he would ever survive prison. Foolish question, he thought, what difference did it make, at my age I'd be a very old man by the time I was free, even if I got out early for good behavior.

"But don't panic yet," Joanna Thorndike said with an encouraging smile. "Anyone could have slipped up that back stairwell while you were in the parking lot, so you're only a person of interest right now, not a full blown suspect."

"That seems like a fine distinction."

"Not so fine. It's the difference between freedom and having to make bail."

"I see," he said softly, shaken.

"If you think of anything that you haven't told us, please get in touch. And don't leave town without contacting me." Thorndike gave him her card. "Have a nice day."

Charles nodded, wondering if she was employing irony.

Chapter Four

W hen Charles got home, he found he was ravenous. He quickly made two peanut butter and jelly sandwiches and ate them with a large glass of milk. He wondered afterwards whether this was a childish reversion to comfort food. He was glad that the Lieutenant didn't know he had such a good appetite because it would probably be another nail in his coffin. Most murderers probably enjoyed a hardy meal after dispensing with their victims.

Thinking of the Lieutenant, he found that, although in one way she terrified him, in another way he was rather attracted to her. She was intelligent with a sly sense of humor, and there was something appealing about her definitely womanly body being wrapped in a quasi-military uniform. He wondered for a moment whether he had some kind of perverted wish to be dominated by a strong woman. Then he wondered if the attraction had something to do with her being so unlike Barbara, who was short and thin with a tendency to wear diaphanous skirts.

People had tried to set him up on dates several times after his year of mourning had ended, but without success. Even when he agreed to go along on an outing, the effort required in meeting a new person with the intention of deepening the relationship made him feel weary, as if he were being asked to climb a steep hill shouldering a heavy rucksack containing the past. His daughter, Amy, had recently suggested that he join an online dating service, perhaps finding one that specialized in people who were difficult to match. Stung, Charles asked her what she meant by that, she had responded with an airy, "Oh, you know."

Thinking about Amy reminded him that he should inform her of the recent turn of events in his life. Even though it was the middle of the day, he could call her at home because she was a full-time homemaker with two small children. Barbara had always worked, even when Amy was small, and Charles often wondered if Amy's decision to stop working as soon as she'd had her first child was somehow an implied criticism of how she had been raised. Although he often wondered about it, Charles knew better than to bring it up with her. Too much honesty between parent and child was never a good thing. His own father's blunt honesty had taught him that.

Amy's husband, Jack, was a high-flying fianancier in Boston, so they could easily survive, even in the expensive Boston area, on one income. Charles thought of him, unkindly, as Jack the Philistine because he'd been a business major and had gone right on to law school with the sole intention of working in finance, although Charles knew that this was somewhat unfair to the Philistines, since recent research showed they had actually been much more cultured than their Israelite enemies, their bad reputation only the price of being on the losing side of history. Amy, on the other had, had received a fine education in history at Opal, and she had gotten in based on merit, not because her father was on the faculty. Sometimes he thought there would be less conflict between them today if she had gone elsewhere and lived away at an earlier age.

He called Amy, and when she answered, he calmly and clearly gave her a summary of his day so far.

"Well, I realize it was an awful shock to you, but I think it's wonderful that you're retiring. Maybe you could move out here and be closer to us," she said, completely skipping over the fact that he'd found a dead body in his office.

"Possibly," he said in a neutral voice, knowing that he didn't really want to leave Opalsville, and he certainly didn't want to be any closer to Boston.

"If it's keeping your hand in teaching you're worried about, I'm sure there would be a college around here that would be happy to take you on as an adjunct."

"I think perhaps my teaching days are over."

"You could always take some time to think about it while visiting Uncle Wally in Florida."

His father's younger brother Walter spent most of his time on his boat, but for Charles, fishing was his idea of having nothing left to do in life. You fish and then you die. Wally, in his early eighties was proof of that point.

"I suppose I could. But I think you're missing the point here, Honey, my retirement is unimportant compared to the fact that I'm a murder suspect."

"Did you kill him?" she asked bluntly.

"No, of course not." He wondered what she really thought of him that she could even ask such a question. Was he really such a mysterious entity, even to his nearest and dearest?

"Then I don't think you have anything to worry about. Things may be a little stressful right now, but it sounds like this guy was the sort who would have lots of enemies. I'm sure a more likely suspect will turn up before too long."

"I hope so."

"Why don't you come out and visit for a few days? The boys would be thrilled to see you."

"Sorry, I've been ordered by the police to stay in town until the investigation is complete."

That wasn't precisely true. Thorndike had asked him to notify her if he left town. But he felt it was close enough to being accurate that he could hide behind it to avoid a prolonged visit. He loved his grandsons deeply, but one day with the boys, now that Barbara wasn't around to share the burden, left him weary and exhausted. Spending more time than that would have him wondering how he had ever been able to raise a child of his own in the first place, and heartily wishing that he hadn't.

Putting Amy off with a vague promise to get back to her when the situation had changed, he hung up. As he sat for a minute on the sofa, reflecting on how many changes retirement was going to make in his life, even if he managed to stay out of prison, he realized that he had promised to deliver his retirement letter today, and had not yet done so. He went into his study in the back of the house, turned on his computer, and wrote a simple, unadorned letter stating his retirement. He read it over carefully; making sure that it didn't contain a hint of either sarcasm or regret. When he was done, he locked up the house and drove over to campus.

He parked in his usual space behind the English building before realizing that he no longer had an office there. He could go in the department office and pick up his mail, but he wasn't certain what kind of reception he'd receive. Would his colleagues shrink back at that sight of him as if he were already wearing an orange jump suit and shackles? Had he been indicted, tried and found guilty by those who knew him best?

Deciding not to find out, he walked past the English Building, and went directly to the administration offices. Girding up his loins

25

to face any type of reception, he walked into the Dean's Office and stood before the secretary's desk. Lois Michaels looked up at him and smiled.

"How are you today, Charles?" she asked as if she hadn't already seen him this morning.

"Pretty good." He extended the hand holding the letter across her desk. "The Dean wanted my request for retirement by the end of the day."

Her face became troubled as she took the letter.

"Could you wait a few minutes while I run this past the Dean?"

Charles nodded. In under a minute she was back.

"Do you have a moment to talk with Dean Carruthers?"

"I suppose so," Charles said, not sure what there was left to say. The last meeting had seemed pretty conclusive to him.

Lois took him to the door of the Dean's office; Carruthers raced across the room and shook his hand like he was priming a pump.

"Come in, Charles, have a seat."

Charles sat in the same chair as before, but this time the Dean sat right across from him, rather than retreating behind his desk.

"Now what's all this about retiring?" Carruthers asked with a smile.

Charles gave him a puzzled look. "The last time we talked you gave me an ultimatum that either I retire or teach freshman composition for the rest of my professional life," Charles said with growing anger.

The Dean flapped a hand as if dispersing a cloud of knats.

"Circumstances have changed as I'm sure you can understand. Due to Professor Underwood's inability to teach, we are sorely in need of someone to cover our American literature courses. We would very much like you to come out of your almost retirement—so to speak—and teach those classes."

"Doesn't it concern you that I am a person of interest in the police investigation into Underwood's murder?"

The Dean flinched at the use of the word *murder*. "You didn't kill him did you?" he asked.

"No," Charles replied loudly, annoyed that once again someone considered him capable of such an act.

"Well, then, there's no problem," the Dean said with a chuckle.

26

Apparently, Charles thought, people considered him fully capable of murder, but not of lying to conceal it. He had somehow earned a reputation of being potentially violent but thoroughly honest, an interesting combination.

Charles sat for a moment looking at the floor. All he had to do was nod agreement, and everything would return to the way it was before. But, of course it wouldn't, not really, being so summarily dismissed after thirty-five years of loyal service was a breach of trust that could never be forgotten. Also in the short period of time since this morning, he had quickly grown accustomed to the idea of being retired. He wasn't certain why, but a small swell of freedom had developed in a part of his mind, and he was reluctant to stifle it.

"I appreciate your offer, but my retirement stands."

"But why?" Carruthers asked, for once apparently anxious to know the answer to one of his questions.

"Because you were right in saying that I haven't worked up to my usual standard for he last three years. And whatever the cause might be, I have no reason to believe that the future will be any different. So I think it would be best if I left."

"I know your feelings were probably hurt by what happened, but don't cut off your nose to spite your face."

Charles smiled at the old fashioned phrase. He couldn't wait to try it on Yuri, and see how he would mangle it.

"I'm not. I'm actually trying to save face by leaving before my performance gets any worse."

Dean Carruthers paused for a minute; his expression hardened.

"I will, of course, accept your retirement request, but understand that given the changed circumstances, there will no longer be a severance payment of two years salary."

"I wouldn't expect it," Charles said calmly.

He and Barbara had always lived rather frugally considering they were a two-income family. He hadn't needed to travel the world doing research, and she had been paid well for the past eight years as a producer for a local television station across the border in Vermont. Not having had to pay tuition for Amy to attend college, he had a nice nest egg that would easily sustain him for even a lengthy life span.

Carruthers seemed stunned that his threats had failed.

27

"But what will we do with your courses. Who will we get to teach them?"

"Hire someone else as your star."

"All the stars have already been taken in American literature for this year. Plus there are apparently some problems with using an Opal College Chair to cinch the deal. It would have been fine if Underwood had lived, but now . . ."

"Everything would have to be renegotiated?"

Carruthers nodded.

"You can always give the courses to Ernest Ritter, it was his field in graduate school. He's been waiting for decades, hoping I'll kick the bucket, so he can take over my courses."

Carruthers shook his head. "You know Ritter never gives a female student a grade above a C no matter how well she does. The only reason we tolerate him at all is that he teaches medieval literature and early English. Those tiny class are filled with masochists anyway."

Charles shrugged. "Then give them to Andrea and hire an underpaid adjunct to teach her courses."

"We already have too many adjuncts. Parents see that and wonder why tuition keeps skyrocketing."

Charles nodded. "A good question."

He got up from his chair, but the Dean remained seated obviously lost in his calculations on how to rebalance the faculty. He didn't even notice when Charles nodded and left the office.

Charles began walking from the administration building to the parking lot that held his car, trying to focus on the beautiful late spring day. He hoped it would distract him from worrying about being a person of interest in a murder investigation.

Although there were always campus police riding around in their cars searching for parking violators, today he noticed a couple of officers walking a foot patrol on the other side of the campus. No doubt a quick response to the event of the morning.

It was difficult to comprehend how much had happened in one day. He had gone from employed to involuntarily retired then back to almost employed and voluntarily retired. He'd found himself replaced by a flashy pseudo-scholar, and found the dead body of said scholar in the middle of his office. He'd been almost accused of murder, and had his daughter and Dean act as if it was not outside the range of possibility. He wondered what would come next.

As he turned the corner to head toward the English Building, who should he see coming his way but Ernest Ritter. The rather short man was dressed in his usual work outfit, a worn, tight, black suit and dark gray tie. He looked like a seedy mortician. Ritter saw Charles coming and planted himself, small legs apart, right in front of Charles, blocking the sidewalk.

"I hear that you are retiring," he said in a challenging tone.

"Yes, I was being replaced by Garrison Underwood."

"But now that he's dead are you still going to retire or will you be hanging around." Ritter managed to make it sound like Charles was a pervert loitering by a playground.

Charles, amazed at the speed with which the story of the murder had travelled around campus, paused, trying to decide whether to tell Ritter the truth. Although it was tempting to give a vague answer and make him sweat for a while, Charles decided that since honesty was apparently his only public virtue, he should stay with it.

"I am still going to retire." He smiled at the man. "Otherwise you'd probably kill me to get my courses."

Instead of laughing uproariously at the thought, Ritter nodded as if the idea had occurred to him. Charles started to believe that Ritter was like people believed him to be, honest but dangerous. He began to wonder whether Ritter might have killed Garrison and hoped to frame him for the crime. By getting both of them out of the way, he'd have a clear shot at teaching Charles' courses. He expressed that idea to Ritter with a smile, as if it were a joke. Hoping the man's expression would give him away.

Ritter smiled grimly but without obvious signs of guilt. "That would have been a brilliant stroke, but unfortunately I wasn't aware of what Yuri and the Dean were up to. That's surprising since Yuri usually leaks information like a colander."

"You hadn't heard about Garrison coming on board?"

"Not a word. As far as I know, no one in the department had any warning."

Charles remembered that Andrea said she knew, so he doubted the truth of what Ritter was saying.

"When the Dean asked me who should take over my courses, I did mention your name," Charles said.

"That's very decent of you, given that we've never exactly been friends."

"But when the Dean expressed reluctance, I suggested that Andrea might take them over."

"Andrea? That girl is no scholar. Has she even written anything in the field?"

"Five articles, and a book is on the way."

"Everyone has a book on the way. It doesn't count until you can see and hold it."

"And what have you done in American literature?" Charles asked, knowing the answer.

"That's hardly a fair question. I've spent the last twenty years teaching medieval literature and Beowulf because you've had the field of American literature sewed up. All my research has had to be in those areas."

"That means the last time you actually studied the scholarship in American was when you were in graduate school two decades ago. A lot has changed since then. Andrea is up to date on all that stuff."

"Nonsense. I deserve those courses because of the time I've put in here."

Charles smiled a bit maliciously. "And I didn't deserve to be replaced by Garrison after thirty-five years. I wouldn't have much confidence in the argument from seniority if I were you."

Ritter turned red. "We'll just see about that. I'm going to have a talk with the Dean right now. They can't treat me shabbily and get away with it."

With that he turned on his heel and marched off in the direction of the administration building.

Charles smiled to himself as he walked back to his car. It wasn't often that he could ruin both Ritter and the Dean's day at the same time.

Chapter Five

Charles woke up at the sound of the alarm and was surprised to see that it wasn't pitch black in his bedroom. Daylight was already peeking around the edge of the shade. Greg Wasserman had called him last night to remind him about their scheduled run in the morning. Although Charles wanted to skip it, he couldn't think of anything else he would be doing at that hour that would serve as an excuse, sleeping somehow didn't cut it. Maybe in his heart of hearts, Charles thought, as he searched around for a sweatshirt and running shorts in the bottom of his dresser, he knew this wasn't a half bad idea. While attending Amherst he'd played on the baseball team, and he recalled those years with pleasure. Perhaps part of the reason for the fond memories was the physical training involved.

Once dressed, Charles went downstairs and looked out the living room window. Wasserman was already in his driveway doing a series of complicated stretches that Charles hoped he didn't have to imitate because they would put him in the hospital. Taking a deep breath, he plastered a smiled on his face and went outside.

"Good morning," Charles said, dancing from foot-to-foot as though anxious to get started, although it was really due to the morning chill on his bare legs.

Greg nodded. "Ready to go?"

"How many miles are we running?"

"How long since you ran last?"

Charles thought back. "Probably thirty years."

Greg gave him a knowing smile and started to run. Charles ran along next to him, exhilarating in the morning air, the sight of the rising sun, and the slap of his shoes on the concrete. He checked his pace to stay next to Greg, although he could have run faster. How hard can this be? he thought.

At the end of the fourth block he began to feel a burning in his chest that made him wonder if he was experiencing a heart attack, by the end of block five his lungs were burning like those of a three-pack-a-day smoker walking up five flights of stairs, and by the end of the sixth block he had a stitch in his side that he was sure indicated a ruptured spleen.

"I can't go on," he gasped, staggering to a halt.

Greg stopped but continued running in place.

"I'm surprised you made it this far. Conditioning only lasts a short while after you stop exercising, and you've been out of shape for years. I'm going to continue on. Why don't you walk back home? We'll get together again tomorrow morning. You'll start to see improvement pretty quickly."

Not trusting himself to speak, Charles nodded, and began the walk of shame back to his house. When he played baseball, he recalled he could run forever. Now he couldn't have run to catch a bus. Maybe the Dean was wrong and all parts of him were deteriorating at the same rapid pace.

A car pulled up next to him. It was a nondescript sedan with Lieutenant Thorndike at the wheel. He stopped when she rolled down the window.

"You don't look so good. Do you want a ride?"

"No, thanks. I was out for a run. I'm just cooling down."

"How far did you run?"

"A little too far."

She smiled, and Charles felt she saw right through him.

"Since we happened to meet like this, would you have a few minutes to talk with me? I wanted to run a new angle on the case past you to see what you thought."

"Aren't I a suspect?"

"Only a person of interest."

"Ah, yes, that subtle distinction. Okay, my house is just up the road."

"I know where it is. I'll meet you there."

Five minutes later Charles walked up the driveway of his house. The Lieutenant was parked in his driveway leaning against the trunk of her car watching him.

"Would you like to come in for a cup of coffee?" he asked.

"A cop who eats donuts would never pass up a cup of coffee."

Charles smiled. He opened the side door and they went into the kitchen. While Charles put the coffee on and went to change, he heard her wandering around the kitchen and the adjacent living room taking in everything like a potential homebuyer.

"What a nice home," she said as he handed her a cup of coffee, "and everything is so neat. You're not the traditional sloppy bachelor."

"I was married for a long time. Domesticity rubbed off on me."

Thorndike leaned against the kitchen counter and studied him.

"When did your wife die?"

"Three years and two months ago."

"What was the cause?"

"A car accident on a snowy evening coming back from her job in Vermont."

She nodded as if this somehow made sense.

"Are you married?" Charles asked.

She shook her head. "Divorced. I have two grown children living in different parts of the country."

"I have a daughter near Boston."

She took another sip of coffee and smiled like she found the place comforting. Charles could believe it. He always did.

Finally she sighed as if coming back to reality.

"What I wanted to run by you is whether the murderer could have been intending to kill you rather than Underwood? After all, he was in your office. Your name was still on the door."

"You mean someone who didn't know me by sight wants to kill me?"

"It's possible if someone was hired to do the job."

Charles laughed. "Who would hire a professional killer to murder an English professor?"

"Given any bad grades lately?" she asked with a smile. Then she went on more seriously. "Do you have any serious enemies?"

Charles gave the question some thought.

"As one gets older a man is more inclined to wonder if he has any real friends who would help him in a time of need. Enemies were more a younger man's luxury. I'm sure there are some people who dislike me more than others, but I doubt anyone feels strongly enough about it to want to take my life."

"Who would gain by your death?"

"My daughter inherits of course. Someone on the faculty would have moved into my slot and gotten to teach my American literature courses."

She smiled. "That doesn't seem like much of a motive."

"That's because you don't teach college. Ernest Ritter has been waiting twenty years to teach my courses. He's a cold, calculating little man—

"But he knows who you are."

"However it's more complicated than that. What if he heard about Underwood coming? Underwood is younger than I am by twenty-five years and younger than Ritter by fifteen. Ritter might outlast me, but he'd most likely never outlast Underwood. So he decides to kill Underwood in such a way as to put the blame on me. In one stroke he gets my courses."

Joanne thought about it. "Possible. But it seems awfully complicated."

"And when I accused him of it, he didn't look guilty."

"You *told* him your theory."

"Sure. I thought if I watched his face I might know if he had done it."

"Did it work?"

"Not really."

"It's usually better to gather a little evidence before accusing someone."

Charles blushed. "I suppose you're right."

"But I will check into Ritter' whereabouts at the time of Underwood's death.

"Thanks." He didn't know if the Lieutenant was just saying that to make him feel better, but he appreciated it.

Is there anyone else who would want you dead?"

Charles shook his head.

They stood there in the kitchen silently drinking their coffee, and Charles realized how nice it was to have a woman in the house, even if it was someone who considered him a person of interest only in a non-romantic sense.

"Were there any other faculty in their offices on the fourth floor at the time of Underwood's death?"

The Lieutenant took out her notebook.

"Andrea Boyd was in her office with the door closed and didn't hear anything. Otherwise the floor was empty."

"Dean Carruthers offered me my job back."

She looked at him sharply. "Did you take it?"

Charles shook his head. "I turned him down."

"Why?"

"I'm not completely sure. I guess I've gotten comfortable with the idea of being retired."

"That happened fast."

Charles sipped his coffee. "I guess I didn't realize how tired I've gotten of teaching. I think I've gradually been losing my enthusiasm for it since Barbara died."

Thorndike nodded. "Trying something new can't hurt. At least it won't have all the old associations."

The Lieutenant finished her coffee, rinsed out her cup, and put it on the drain board next to the sink.

"Am I still a person of interest?" Charles asked.

She smiled. "Not a much as you would have been if you took back your old job. Then it would have looked as though you killed Underwood to get his job. Not taking it weakens the case against you or else it proves that you're one very smart murderer who's playing some kind of deep game."

"Is that really likely?"

"I don't know, Charles. You're not easy to figure."

"I've recently learned that I'm somewhat inscrutable even to my daughter."

"Everybody hides things, even from their nearest and dearest. But the good news for now is that you can remove your personal effects from your old office. We've gone through everything. And if you do think of anyone who might be out to get you, let me know."

"I will."

With a smile and a nod, Thorndike walked out the side door.

Charles remained standing in the kitchen for a moment realizing that he had experienced a real senses of loss when Thorndike left the house. He wasn't sure what attracted him to her. Maybe it was her sense of humor or her strong physical presence. Was that just a fancy way of saying he liked her body? Charles wondered, always wanting to be honest with himself about things like that.

He poured himself a bowl of cereal and, managing to balance that and his coffee in one hand; he opened the back door and went out on the patio to eat. He looked at the pool that his wife had always enjoyed, which he now religiously maintained although he never went in it. He thought about how he didn't want to move nearer his daughter or go back to teaching. But a life spent sitting around the house after the habitual morning run sounded lonely and limited. He could, of course, read *The New York Times* carefully from front to back, but having too much time and being fully informed was what he thought made most seniors cranky. He wondered if he was lonely already and wasn't sure he was. He was alone, but being lonely required a desire for the company of others. He wasn't confident that he was willing to disturb the still waters of his life by allowing someone else into it.

After finishing his breakfast, he decided to go into the college and pick up his possessions from the office. He went into the bathroom, looked in the mirror and saw his face was covered with dark stubble mixed with flecks of gray. He wondered what The Lieutenant had made of that. Probably not much, he decided. When you're thirty, stubble is sexy; when you're over sixty, it just makes you look homeless, he thought, lathering up.

Chapter Six

As Charles climbed up the flights of stairs to his office, using the back staircase as usual, he thought about having had the same office for over thirty-five years, of all the articles and the two critically acclaimed books he'd written there, of the time when he and Barbara has finished a couple of bottles of wine there while celebrating his promotion to full professor and gotten amorous. The realization came, like a sharp pain in his side, that he would miss the place, even the smell of dust and old wood that permeated the air.

When he reached his office, he noticed right away that the door was ajar. Was there any truth to the notion that murderers return to the scenes of their crimes? For a moment he considered going to the English Department office and asking the secretary to accompany him inside. But that sounded awfully craven, and since he was a person of interest, she probably wouldn't be willing to go anywhere with him alone.

He slowly opened the door, thankful that he had oiled the hinges a few weeks ago. A woman was standing with her back to him, surveying the room. He cleared his throat, and she spun around, pressing a hand to her ample chest. Charles estimated she was in her late thirties.

"Who are you?" she asked.

"I'm Charles Bentley and this is my office. Or at least it used to be."

She nodded matter-of-factly. "You're the one they say killed my husband. Over a job."

"Not really. I mean, I didn't kill him."

She reached out her hand and Charles shook it briefly. He was amazed at how civilized she was being. Perhaps the British really were different, he thought admiring her stylish clothes and erect stance.

"I'm Sylvia Underwood. And I wouldn't blame you if you had killed Garrison. He could be a thoroughgoing bastard at times. He cheated on me from when we were first married. I should have known that he would, after all he slept with me when I was his graduate assistant, and he was still married to his first wife. Why should I have believed that he'd be any more faithful to me?" She gave a short laugh. "Women always have high hopes that they can reform a serial philanderer. Foolish optimism."

"Who do you think killed him?" Charles asked, slowly recovering from the barrage of information given in a plummy accent.

"I'd put my money on that last girlfriend of his. She was stupid enough to get pregnant, and was suing him for alimony and child support. That's why Garrison took off for the states, to try to get away from her. I told him it wouldn't work. I saw her once and you could see the tenacity etched into her cute little face. You know, it's ironic; Garrison and I wanted to get pregnant and never had any luck. Then this tart comes along and all he has to do it look at her."

"I'm sure he did more than that," Charles observed.

Sylvia grinned. "I'm sure he did."

"Is this latest girlfriend in this country?"

"I wouldn't be surprised, she fixed on Garrison like a limpet. Like I said, that was the only reason he came over here. Garrison really didn't like the states. We were here for a while about ten years ago, right after we got married, but it didn't work out very well."

"Why not?"

"There were several reasons, but I think the fundamental reason was that he didn't like it here: too much competition. The field of English scholarship is much smaller back in the U.K. Everyone more or less knows everyone, and it's easy to establish a reputation. The pool over here is many times larger, and I think Garrison liked being a larger fish in a smaller pond."

"You mentioned that his girlfriend might have killed him. Wouldn't that be counterproductive for her? She wouldn't be able to sue a dead man."

"Oh, she'll still try to get something from his estate I'm sure. And you're assuming she's rational. The one time I met her she as crazy with anger towards him. She's capable of anything."

"Is there anyone else who might be a suspect?"

Sylvia Underwood smiled and seemed to stand even taller. "I'm probably a likely candidate; after all, I get to inherit. The royalties from his books together with his life insurance should add up to a tidy sum. Plus I'll have my freedom. To be honest it feels like the end of a twelve year prison sentence."

"Couldn't you have gotten quite a bit of money and your freedom by just divorcing him?"

"He'd have fought me tooth and nail simply on the principal of the thing. He didn't like to give up anything that belonged to him. And he knew a lot of solicitors, former students of his, who would have represented him for free. He'd have managed to throw me out with nothing."

"And now you have it all. That does give you a motive."

"Yes. I have lots of motive, but no opportunity. I spent all of yesterday with a realtor looking for a place where we could live. That female police lieutenant has already checked it out."

"I hope you haven't had a lot of possessions shipped over already," Charles said.

"No, mostly clothes and some things Garrison wanted in his office. In fact that's why I'm here. The police said I could gather up the items Garrison left beind. Would you help me sort them out, so I don't take anything that belongs to you?"

Charles nodded at the box on the floor.

"Your husband had already disposed of my things."

Sylvia Underwood smiled grimly. "Garrison was always quick to take over wherever he went."

With Charles' help they soon had her late husbands pictures off the walls and the desk emptied. They packed it all in a cardboard box Sylvia had brought with her.

"Not much to show for a man's life," she said, hefting the box.

"I'm sure his real legacy is in his books and the minds of his students."

She nodded and Charles thought he detected a tear in the corner of her eye.

"For all the bad qualities Garrison had, he could be magical at times. He had a truly fine mind."

Charles nodded, reserving his own opinion.

She shook his hand again and thanked him for his help.

"I'll probably see you again. The police don't want me to go home just yet."

With a final smile she lifted up the box and left the room.

Charles gave her a few minutes head start. He picked up his own box, gave his office one last long sentimental look, then carefully locked the office door and went down the back stairs.

As he put the box in the trunk of his car, Charles noticed a streak of dirt on the side of his car that had survived the car wash of two days ago and used his handkerchief to rub it off.

"Don't give in to your O.C.D.," a voice said behind him.

He looked over his shoulder and saw Andrea Boyd grinning at him.

"Obsessive compulsives do most of the world's great work. They're the only ones who care enough to get it right," Charles responded.

Andrea laughed in that free and open way that made Charles heart skip a beat. Fool! Old fool! He warned himself.

"Have you heard anything from the Dean about teaching my courses?" he asked.

"I got a call from Yuri this morning. Apparently he and the Dean discussed it, and I'll be doing your seventeenth century American literature course. Ernest will have eighteenth."

"You should have gotten them both."

Andrea shrugged. "At least I have one less freshmen composition."

"I'm sure Ritter will be livid that he didn't get both of them."

"I just ran into him. He accused me of using my feminine wiles to influence the Dean and Yuri to give me that course. Even if I had any wiles to use, I think they'd be wasted on those two."

"Ritter, like most misogynists, is fixated on women's sexuality and greatly exaggerates their power."

"Couldn't you talk to the Dean and get him to let you teach the course he gave to Ritter? I hate the thought of having him ruin the minds of young people particularly for American literature."

"The Dean offered me my old job back, but I refused."

"Why did you do that?" she asked, aghast.

Charles looked across the parking lot to the row of spruce trees beyond. He dug deeper to see if he could give Andrea a more accurate answer than he had given Lieutenant Thorndike.

"I think that Barbara's death put a punctuation mark to one period of my life. I didn't realize it at the time and carried on in a listless way with my previous activities. Being forced to retire suddenly made me realize that I want to do something different with my life. I don't want to drift into old age merely following familiar habits."

"But you could teach one course and still do other things. The Dean would probably be happy to take that course away from Ritter and give it to you."

"Once you leave the party, you don't slip back in again by the rear door."

"I don't know why not," she said, obviously annoyed. "I hate the idea of not having you on the faculty anymore. You're one of the few people I can relate to."

"We can still see each other."

"But it won't be the same."

Charles shrugged. "I'm starting to realize that nothing stays the same, even those things that you think have."

"Has the police investigation of Underwood's death revealed anything so far?"

"I don't think so. The Lieutenant said you'd been questioned because you were in your office at the approximate time of Underwood's death."

"Unfortunately, I had my door closed and didn't see or hear anything. I wish I could give you an alibi for at least part of that half hour."

"No problem. I may be off the hook anyway. Lieutenant Thorndike is now speculating that I might have been the intended victim. But the hired goon—if that's what you'd call him—killed the wrong person by mistake."

Andrea looked concerned. "You don't have any enemies that would put a contract out on you, do you?"

"I doubt that anyone cares for me so strongly either way, except for Amy."

He heard how pathetic that sounded and immediately regretted his words.

"C'mon, Charles, I care for you."

"Thank you. And I wasn't fishing for emotional support. I'm afraid I sometimes give in to feeling sorry for myself."

"We all do," Andrea said seriously.

"The other thing I just found out is that Underwood's wife is in town. Sylvia Underwood was just up in my office picking up her husband's things. She would have gained a great deal by killing him, but apparently she has an alibi for the time of his death."

"Interesting, well I guess I'd better get going," Andrea said abruptly. "I have some grocery shopping to do on my way home. We'll have to get together for that dinner. I'll give you a call."

"I'd like that."

Charles watched her walk away, moving quickly with the bouncy step of what seemed to him like youth. And he reminded himself once again that some dreams just aren't meant to be.

Chapter Seven

Back home Charles ate a tuna fish sandwich and heated up the morning coffee. Since Barbara died, he found he had lost weight, probably because his own cooking was somewhat rudimentary, but more likely because dinner times were no longer cheerful occasions for sharing the events of the day. Fortunately, he hadn't turned to alcohol as a substitute for food, the way he'd heard some other widowed and divorced men of his age did. He knew what he needed waas a new life, not just a temporary anesthetizing.

A new life without work, it wouldn't feel strange in the summer because he'd always had those free, but he wondered what he would experience in the fall when the cool breezes began to blow and the leaves started to turn. Wouldn't it seem strange not to be able to chart the season in relation to the semester's work? But the more immediate problem was what would he do right now? Even though he'd had summers off from teaching, he generally used them as a period for intense writing and research. But he'd lost that focus over the last three years, and now he had no reason at all to return to scholarship. He was completely at loose ends.

Pushing such big life questions aside, he took a cup of the reheated coffee and *The New York Times* out on the patio with him. For the moment at least he'd catch up on the news and watch the pool ripple. He'd started to doze off when the doorbell rang fifteen minutes later. He rose stiffly and walked down the hall. Opening the door, he found Lieutenant Thorndike standing on the front porch.

"Sorry to bother you twice in the same day," she said.

"No bother. Unless you've come to arrest me."

Thorndike smiled. "Not this time."

They went into the kitchen and Charles offered her a cup of reheated coffee.

"Even reheated its better than what I get at the station," she said.

"I was out on the patio. There's a nice breeze there now."

"Let's go."

They sat next to each other looking out across the pool and the lawn beyond.

"Do you use the pool much?" Thorndike asked.

"Never. It was more my wife's thing. I can't see the point in getting wet just to get dry again."

"But I can see you keep it clean."

"I keep everything clean."

"I've noticed that what I've seen of your house looks spotless."

Charles nodded. "I can be a bit of a clean and neatness freak. It used to drive Barbara crazy. She'd put something down in the wrong spot for a minute, then reach for it to find I'd put it away."

"That might bother me, too. But neatness in a husband isn't such a bad thing. My ex would let his dirty clothes lie wherever he dropped them. I guess he thought there were elves that provided him with clean clothes every week. Of course, that was the least of his problems."

"There are worse things. I met Sylvia Underwood today. Apparently her husband was chronically unfaithful to her."

"I had a chat with her as well. Sounds like a marriage that would drive a wife to kill. Unfortunately she has a solid alibi for the time of death."

"Maybe she hired someone to do it," Charles suggested.

"She'd probably have had it done in England then, rather than over here."

"I've been thinking about that hired killer scenario with regard to the murderer being after me. And I doubt a hired killer would rely on finding something on the spot to hit his victim over the head with. He'd probably bring a gun or knife."

"I agree. In fact the reason I came over here was to tell you that the trophy had been wiped clean of prints, so yours weren't on it. That makes you less of a suspect because I doubt you'd have volunteered that you handled it if you'd already wiped it clean."

"Unless I'm playing a deep game," Charles said with a smile.

"There is that," Thorndike agreed cheerfully. "One other thing is that Underwood was hit on the back of the head, so most likely the attack came from someone he knew. We don't usually turn our backs on strangers."

"I'm not so sure of that. Underwood impressed me as the kind of guy who would turn his back on anyone as a sign of disdain.

Thorndike thought about that for a moment and nodded. "Especially if the other person was a woman, and he didn't feel threatened."

"Sylvia seemed to believe that his most recent girlfriend is a good candidate for the role of murderer."

"Nora Chapman. I'm going to interview her later on this afternoon. But apparently she only arrived in the country this morning."

"I suppose you're going to check that out."

"Of course."

They sat, companionably drinking their coffee for a couple of minutes.

"What are you going to do now that you've retired for the second and probably last time from Opal College?"

"People keep asking me that, but I have no idea. It worries me that I might not have enough to do."

"Officers I know who have retired are always saying that they're so busy they can't imagine how they found time to work."

"Maybe they have hobbies. For me there was only my work and my family. Now my work is gone, and so is my family," he replied gloomily.

"You could visit your daughter more."

Charles made a face. "She has her own life. What would you do if you retired?"

"Visit my sons once in a while. Otherwise, I'm not sure. I like my job, so I never give it much thought."

"You could always get together with the people still on the force that you know."

She shook her head. "Once you're off the force, you drop out of the conversation because you're no longer privy to daily events."

"You could see retired officers. Probably most of them stay in town."

"And reminisce about the past. I'm not sure that's healthy. Do you plan to get together with friends from the faculty?"

"Only Andrea Boyd. She's been a friend of Barb's and mine for a long time. Otherwise, I guess not. A faculty isn't a team like the police; they're more independent contractors. We don't exactly have each other's backs the way cops do. The camaraderie is much looser."

"Don't you get any guidance on how to live from all those books you read?" asked Thorndike. "I would think the great writers talked a lot about the big issues of life."

"Nineteenth century novels can be helpful in that regard, but from the twentieth century on most protagonists are struggling unsuccessfully to find solutions to the problems of life."

"Sounds depressing."

"That's what makes great literature."

They sat there for a moment considering that. Finally, the Lieutenant got up to leave. Charles walked her to the door.

"Well, thank you for letting me know about the lack of fingerprints. I feel slightly less threatened."

She smiled. "I wanted to let you know right away."

Charles wondered why she hadn't just given him a call, but he didn't ask because he didn't want to embarrass her in case she had simply wanted to see him. And if that wasn't the reason, why spoil his dream that it might have been true.

Chapter Eight

T he next morning the alarm woke him at six-thirty for another run—so to speak—with Greg Wasserman. Greg was out front promptly at seven, and Charles reluctantly joined him. As they started up the street there was none of the euphoria of yesterday. Charles awaited with dread the burning in the lungs and stitch in the side telling him he had reached his limit. Greg had told him it would get better, but although he pretended to agree, Charles secretly believed that these were irreversible signs of aging. The body of his youth was as gone as his full head of hair.

When the gasping and the pain came, Charles had to admit that they weren't as severe as yesterday, and he had managed to run five blocks more than yesterday. Somewhat cheered, he stopped and waved for Greg to continue on. Greg, however, stopped and ran in place.

"My wife, Ruth, will be waiting for you at the sidewalk by your house," Greg said. "She wants to talk to you about working in the soup kitchen. I told her you were retired, and she immediately starting thinking about what you could do with your free time. Ruth's a planner."

He said this as if it were a genetic condition, and stared sadly into the distance as if physicists could see that in the long run all human plans came to nothing.

"Okay. But community service isn't really my thing."

Greg nodded as if he understood but considered the outcome inevitable. "Ruth can be very persuasive."

Turning, Greg continued on his run, and Charles began the walk back home, desperately trying to think of excuses for not working in a soup kitchen that wouldn't make him appear selfish or elitist. He had no objection to welfare projects privately or publically funded, but he had no burning desire to actually participate in them. As he came near his house, he saw Ruth standing by the curb like a crossing guard waiting to escort him to the other side of his life. Squat, with an earth-motherly figure—the physical opposite of her husband—she waved to him as he approached.

"I suppose Greg warned you that I was going to pressure you to work in the soup kitchen."

Charles nodded.

"And for the entire walk back you've been trying to come up with reasons you could give me for not doing so."

Charles nodded guiltily.

Ruth smiled. The smile turned her plain face into something almost beautiful, and Charles caught of glimmer of why Greg had married her.

"I like your honesty. And I want you to know that I didn't think of you just because you aren't working anymore. I don't know you well, but from what I've seen and heard, you've got a good way with people, and you're not stuck up the way so many other faculty are. Also you're not truly eccentric like my Greg, which can be off-putting with strangers."

"Thank you."

He'd always thought he had the common touch. He took pride in thinking it was one of the things making him different from his father. During college, he took humble summer jobs instead of the fancy internships most of his classmates wrangled through family connections. He went into the Army when drafted and did a tour in Vietnam, even though his father thought he was stupid, telling him wasn't some ghetto kid who had no alternative, and he could easily get deferred. Even when Charles came home safe and sound, his father told him his behavior was irresponsible, and it was foolish to risk a life such as his as canon fodder. His father didn't say all this while on some emotional jag, but calmly and eloquently because he honestly believed it.

"What we'd want you to do is set up tables and work the line doling out food," Ruth explained, forcing Charles back into the present. "There is one other man who can help you with the tables, but the rest of the workers are women. We really need another man to help with the heavier work."

So my life of the mind had become a life of the body, Charles thought, not completely unhappy with the idea.

"How often would I do this?"

"Three days a week: Monday, Wednesday and Friday."

Ruth stared at him expectantly while he considered the plan.

"Okay," Charles said, "I'll give it a try."

Charles knew that if he'd declined, Ruth had further arguments up her sleeves she could have produced until it would have been churlish to refuse. Plus a part of him was curious about what his reaction would be to participating actively in charitable work.

"Thanks, Charles, I think you'll find it very rewarding," Ruth said, as if completely certain that to give was better than to receive.

Giving Ruth a parting nod, Charles went up the driveway of his home, picking up the *New York Times* lying there and tucking it under his arm. He went in the side door to the kitchen and poured himself a cup of coffee from the machine he'd put on before he went out to run, and got himself a bowl of cereal. Making two trips he carefully put down a placemat on the patio table and brought out his paper and breakfast.

On a shelf along the back of the house, he had three pots of annuals arranged in a row. Noticing that one seemed out of alignment with the others, and knowing this would bother him constantly, Charles carefully nudged it back in line with the other two. Then he sat down at the table, opened the front section of the *Times*, and began to read.

CRACK!

Charles jumped and heard something fall behind him. Turning, he saw that the flowerpot furthest from him lay in pieces on the ground.

CRACK!

As he watched, the second pot in the row seemed to jump in the air and explode into pieces.

Before the third shot was fired, demolishing the last pot, Charles was moving in a bent over, shambling run toward the door. Once inside the kitchen, he sat on the floor and leaned his cheek against the cool of the lower cabinet door waiting for his heart to slow. He imagined bullets flying by his head, buzzing like angry wasps, as they had in the distant past. After there were several minutes of silence, he crawled into the study on the other side of the house and called the police.

Chapter Nine

Lieutenant Thorndike sat in his kitchen, a cup of coffee in her hand.

"I made fresh," Charles said.

Thorndike smiled. "And I appreciate it. You said that you made sure those pots were in a straight row just before the shots were fired."

Charles nodded.

"I still can't get over how neat everything is around here."

"It's a discipline. A cluttered space makes for a cluttered mind."

"I'll ignore the insult."

"Insult?"

"If you ever saw my office, you'd know that my mind must be a mess."

"I'm only speaking for myself. If the house were untidy, I'd be unable to think."

"So you were right in the line of fire for a minute or so, but the shots didn't begin until you were seated."

"Correct."

"And the one furthest from you went first, then the next. By the time the last one went, you were heading in the door."

"Right. I got out of the way fast because I was the next in the row."

"But there were no further shots once you went in the house."

"None at all."

Thorndike looked out the kitchen window.

"The shots must have come from out along the tree line. My people searched, but they weren't able to find any signs of a shooter out there. But the person could have policed up their brass. We'll talk to your neighbors, but someone could drive up the road and pull into the meadow and easily get away without ever being seen."

Charles nodded.

"I don't imagine you're a hunter. Do you know anything about rifles?"

"I was in the military."

Her eyebrow went up in surprise. "Then you know it would be a pretty easy shot from the wood line to where you were sitting, less than a hundred and fifty feet. And you were a still target, just like those pots."

"So you're saying the shooter could easily have hit me if he wanted to?"

She nodded. "If he'd started with you instead of the pots."

"Why would he intentionally miss?" Charles said, taking a sip of coffee. He was drinking more coffee than he usually did in a day because of Thorndike's visits, and felt slightly jumpy. But he wasn't sure if that was a result of the coffee or getting shot at.

"Perhaps he just wanted to frighten you."

"Why?"

"I don't know. Of course, maybe I'm wrong. Possibly someone wants us to think that you were the real target in the Underwood murder and send us off on a wild goose chase."

"There's the contract killer theory again—I've always thought that was pretty weak. Maybe it was someone who really wanted to kill me, but he was a bad shot."

"He hit the three pots just fine."

"People aren't pots. Maybe he'd never shot a person before and his hands shook."

The Lieutenant thought about that for a moment, then nodded.

"That brings us back to why someone would want to kill you."

"Maybe it's someone who thinks I killed Underwood and wants revenge."

"Who?"

"His wife."

"You've met her?"

Charles nodded.

"Then you know she isn't exactly heartbroken by his death."

"Maybe there's someone who wants both Underwood and myself dead."

"Who would that be?"

"Ernest Ritter."

Thorndike rolled her eyes. "Okay, I asked him about his whereabouts at the time of the murder, and he says he was on his way into the college when Underwood was killed. Of course, there was no way I can really check on that. But I will talk with him and find out about where he was this morning today if it will make you feel better."

Charles shrugged. "It's hard to imagine Ritter committing a double homicide. He seems more a talker than a doer. But he is the only one with a motive to have Underwood and I both off the scene. I guess there could be two people: one who killed Underwood and the other who wants to kill me."

"Have you ever heard of Occam's razor?" asked Thorndike.

"Sure, it's a principle that says always go with the simplest hypothesis that covers the facts."

"Well, I try to follow that. And two shooters is definitely not the simplest explanation of what has happened. Unless something different happens in the future to change my mind, we're assuming one murderer. Okay?"

"Okay."

"Just play it safe. Stay inside and don't go out unless you have to."

"I'm working in the soup kitchen at St. David's."

Her eyebrows went up. "When did this start?"

"Today. My next door neighbor, Ruth Wasserman, talked me into it this morning."

Thorndike sighed. "No problem, you'll be around lots of other people, that should keep you safe."

The Lieutenant got up and walked to the door. She stopped in the doorway and turned to Charles.

"Are you sure you're all right. Not too shaken up."

"No, I'm fine."

"You've been shot at before?"

He nodded.

She gave him a long look, then left.

Charles stood there staring at across the road for a few minutes wondering how he really did feel about being shot at for the first time in forty years. He was surprised to find that he felt very angry. Whether the intention was to kill or only frighten, Charles considered that the action had changed things. With Underwood's death, his interest had been primarily to avoid being blamed, but now he felt that the killer had directly involved him in the matter. It was time for him to see what he could do to discover the identity of the murderer.

52

Easier said than done, he thought. He didn't have any special skills at detecting. However, he reminded himself, scholarship was a matter of sifting evidence and finding support for a conclusion. These skills could easily be adapted to discovering who had murdered Underwood. He would go out and gather date, then subject it to rigorous analysis.

He took a deep breath, and felt more determined than he had since Barbara's death. He might not have cared for the murdered man, but now their fates were inextricably linked.

Chapter Ten

Charles pulled into the parking lot of Saint David's Episcopal Church, and parked in a row of cars near the door. An arrow saying "Soup Kitchen" pointed in the direction of the basement, and he followed it down. There were noises at the far end of the basement, and he found his way into the kitchen. A group of about five women were working away, feverishly preparing food. Charles went up to the woman talking loudest, who had a natural air of command, and introduced himself.

"Hi, I'm Nancy," she said, reaching out to shake his hand. Realizing she was wearing an oven mitt, she waved instead. "You'll be setting up the tables with John as soon as he gets here."

"If he gets here," a younger woman muttered.

Nancy smiled weakly. "John has several health issues that make him less than completely reliable."

The younger woman looked up as if she intended to elaborate on that statement, but at a glance from Nancy she changed her mind and returned to her work. Charles was about to ask if there was anything he could do in the meantime when a skinny man wearing a white t-shirt and jeans appeared in the doorway. He shifted nervously from foot-to-foot as if anticipating the need to escape at any minute. Charles pegged him as a guy who did alcohol or drugs instead of food.

"Good morning, ladies," he shouted in a raspy voice.

There was a chorus of disinterested grunts in reply.

"John, this is Charles," Nancy said, pointing her oven mitt in his direction. "He'll be helping you with the tables."

"Well, let's get started then," John said, as if he had been waiting hours for Charles to arrive.

The walked back along the length of the basement to where the tables were stacked against the wall. He went to one end of the stack and Charles to the other.

"We start setting them up at this end and go to the other. They might not seem heavy at first, but by the tenth one you'll start to feel it."

Charles lifted his end of the table and was surprised at how heavy it as. They were older tables with a solid steel construction: heavy but durable. John gave a grunt and lifted his end. Without a moment of hesitation, he directed Charles to where he wanted it placed. They worked steadily and in silence until all the tables were arranged the way John wanted them. Charles could feel the sweat running down his back, and John's face was such a bright red that Charles wondered if he was going to have a heart attack or a stroke. But after he stood leaning against the last table for a minute staring into space, he seemed to get a second wind.

"So what did you do before you started with this?" John asked, as if arranging tables in a soup kitchen had been a career move.

"I taught college."

"At Opal?"

Charles nodded.

"What did you teach?"

"American literature."

John grunted in such a way that Charles wasn't sure whether he approved or didn't approve of the subject.

"So Professor," he said, managing to make the title sound disreputable. "What's your opinion of doing real work?"

Charles wasn't sure how to respond to such a loaded question. Any answer was bound to make it sound like he'd never done any physical labor before that morning.

"It was fine," he said neutrally.

John smirked. "Try doing it for a full day, then a full week, and then a month and see how you like it."

Charles had had enough. "So what sort of work are *you* currently doing?" he asked, figuring he had a pretty good idea of the answer.

John fidgeted and shifted from foot-to-foot.

"I'm between jobs right now. That's why I help out here."

"I see," Charles said, managing to make it sound like he knew exactly why John had no job.

The other man blushed. He looked like he might take a swing at him, so Charles braced himself. Fighting in the soup kitchen on his first day wasn't going to help his reputation.

"Charles we need you to take your place on the line," Nancy said, quickly walking over and standing between the two men. "John, go to the door and tell folks they can start filing in."

Casting a last venomous look at Charles, John headed for the door.

"Don't mind him," Nancy said, taking Charles' arm and guiding him toward the serving tables, where the steaming food was set up in in large bins. "He gets rather aggressive around other men."

Charles thought she made John sound like a dog you wouldn't want to adopt from the pound.

Nancy led him over to the line of women standing behind the food. There was one empty space where she neatly slotted Charles. He looked in front of him and saw an aluminum pan filled to overflowing with mashed potatoes. For some reason the sight of so much food made him feel slightly nauseous.

"Now don't give anyone more than one scoop. Some people will ask for more, especially when they see a new person on the line who they think might be an easy mark. But we have to make sure we don't run out." Nancy stared hard at Charles waiting for a response. He slowly nodded.

"Good. If you have any questions the ladies can help you."

"Don't pay any attention to Nancy," a woman whispered in his left ear once Nancy had walked away. "We only ran out of food once last year, but she was so spooked by it that now she overdoes it, and we're always throwing food away at the end of the day. If somebody asks for more, give it to them if Nancy isn't looking. That's what I do."

Charles looked over at the woman who had spoken to him. She was pleasantly attractive but a bit out of date, like perhaps she had played the lead in a late seventies sitcom and never changed her look. He wondered when it was that pleasantly attractive older women had become his age.

"I'm Karen Melrose," she said, extending a plastic glove covered hand, which Charles shook.

"Have you been doing this long?" he asked, nodding to the row of food.

"Two years ago. I started right after my husband, George, died."

"I'm sorry," Charles said.

Karen nodded. "It was very sudden. I was in the kitchen making dinner. When I came out to the living room to get him, he was on the floor, dead of a massive stroke."

"That must have been a terrible shock."

"Yes. People always say that it was a blessing that he didn't linger in a vegetative state. I suppose that's true, but it might have given me a little time to get used to the whole idea of his being gone."

"My wife died suddenly as well," Charles said, surprised that he mentioned it. He almost never talked about Barbara. It was still too raw.

"How did it happen?"

He felt his throat close up as tears began to sting his eyes.

"Auto accident," he managed to choke out.

Whether Karen could sense that he was barely under control or not, she mercifully didn't ask him any more questions. Soon the line of people arrived, and they were busy doing their respective jobs.

The folks going down the line with plastic plates in hand were mostly men. They effusively thanked the women servers, but barely gave him nod. Perhaps it was because he did not look so much different from them. All were older and, aside from being unshaven in several cases or having gap-toothed expressions from missing teeth, with a little personal care, they would not have looked out of place at an Opal College faculty meeting. And probably they would accomplish more, Charles thought with a silent chuckle.

But slowly a more serious thought began, as the similarity brought home to him how porous was the line between being respectable and being considered a derelict. He told himself that when he got home, he would take a hard look at his retirement account and perhaps make an appointment with his money manager. He had generally ignored the man's calls and solicitations, but that might be foolish now that his well being depended entirely on his investments.

After the lunch rush was over, which was short but fierce, the staff pushed a couple of tables together and sat down to eat what was left of the same food they'd been doling out. Charles was introduced by Nancy to the group as a whole, and everyone nodded politely. The women quickly divided up into several small conversational groupings. He was the only man at the table. John had eaten with some of the men who had come in, and he was now standing just outside the door smoking and chatting with them. Karen was seated next to him, and although she talked sporadically to several women on her left, she frequently made comments to Charles who

57

responded politely. Clearly she wanted him to be involved in the conversation either out of politeness or friendliness.

Charles found that he didn't have much of an appetite, and pushed the food around on his plate, barely eating any. He thought it might have been because he rarely ate very much for lunch.

"The smell of the food puts you off eating," Karen said with authority.

"Why is that?" he asked. "The food is all good, isn't it?"

"Of course, but I think the smell might be a substitute for eating. In some strange way the aroma fills you up."

Charles thought about that for a moment.

"Maybe the part of your brain that makes you hungry becomes numbed by all the smells."

"Could be. A friend of mine came up from the south last week and brought me several pints of blueberries. Do you like blueberry crumble?"

"Sure, I think so," Charles replied. He vaguely remembered Barbara had made something with blueberries, but whether it was a crumble or cobbler, he couldn't recall.

Karen smiled and nodded. "Are you going to be back tomorrow?"

He shook his head. "I'm only on three days a week. I won't be back until Friday."

Karen looked disappointed. "Will you really be coming back?"

"Why wouldn't I?" he asked in surprise.

She shrugged. "Most men come once, and never return."

"Why do you think that is?"

"I think it's because they're not in charge of anything. Men like to be in charge, you know. They don't adjust well to just being another worker. And men don't get much thanks from our clients."

"Clients?"

"That's what Nancy wants us to call the people we feed."

"Well, I noticed that the men seemed to thank the women more than me."

"Another man makes them feel ashamed of what's happened to them. Being successful, you make them feel even more like a failure."

Charles thought for a moment. "There's not much I can do about that."

"I don't suppose there is. Just be nice to them, and eventually they'll get used to you."

A firm hand came down on his shoulder and John stuck his face in his. Charles could smell the stench of cigarette smoke and a hint of beer.

"Time to take down the tables, Professor, if you still feel up to it."

As Charles stood, he turned to Karen, "Don't worry, I'll be back," he said, certain he would, but not really sure why.

Chapter Eleven

It was the middle of the afternoon when Charles got home. He thought for a long moment about sitting out on the patio on the assumption that the shooter was unlikely to visit twice on the same day, but then he thought how angry Lieutenant Thorndike would be if he got shot right after she had warned him to be careful. Angry and, he hoped, a little bit sad.

With a sigh he went into his study and sat behind his desk. He looked at the desktop, covered with the remains of abandoned projects, and he felt like a captain at the helm of a ghost ship. He thought for one liberating moment about sweeping the desk clean, and throwing all the detritus of the past few years into the garbage bin and starting life anew.

But old habits died hard, and his mind drifted back to a time when he and Barbara shared happy times together on the long summer nights. His reverie was interrupted by a knock on the front door. He walked out into the hall and opened the door. Andrea stood there studying him anxiously.

"Are you okay?"

"Of course. Why shouldn't I be?"

"I heard that someone took a shot at you this morning."

Charles directed her into the living room, and took a seat across from where she was perched on the sofa.

"Where did you hear that?"

"The security guard at the college heard it from someone on the police."

"Word spreads fast," he said, thinking that Thorndike wouldn't be happy to discover police lips weren't tightly sealed.

"Is it true?"

"Well, there's some dispute over whether the person was actually shooting at me. The only casualties were three flower pots."

"But you were out there at the time, right?"

"True. The question is whether the perpetrator was shooting at me and missed, which is extremely unlikely given the distance, or whether he was attempting to make it appear that I was the real target from the start rather than Underwood. In that way possibly diverting the police investigation."

"That last theory is very clever," said Andrea.

"And probably the most likely. If the police thought I was meant to be the original victim, they'd stop focusing on Underwood's life and look at mine, which has been almost utterly blameless."

Andrea smiled. "I think you underestimate yourself. I'm sure there are a few skeletons in your closet."

"If so, they've gathered a lot of dust over many years, whereas I suspect Underwood's are still fresh, dancing around clean and shiny."

Andrea looked around. "Speaking of clean and shiny, you keep this house in tiptop shape."

"Lieutenant Thornton said the same thing earlier today."

"Has she been coming around harassing you? Does she still insist on thinking of you as a suspect?"

Charles wondered if Andrea was only concerned about police harassment or whether she was a bit jealous of the Lieutenant. But he quickly dismissed that idea as a geriatric delusion.

"I was never a suspect, merely a person of interest. And I think I may even be leaving that list rather shortly."

"I should hope so."

Andrea took another glance around the room.

"Keeping everything clean is fine, Charles, but you've also kept it exactly as it was when Barbara was alive. It's like a museum in here."

Charles shrugged. "I see no reason to rearrange things just for the sake of variety. The way we had them is the way that suits me." He knew he sounded prim and fussy, but it was the truth.

"But now that you're retired you can't just sit around here all day remembering the past. It's not healthy. Why don't you ask the Dean to give back one of the courses he transferred to Ritter. I'm sure he'd be more than happy to do it."

"Like I said, when I'm done, I'm done. My time at Opal College has come to an end."

Andrea shook her head in frustration. "You can be incredibly stubborn at times."

"I worked at the soup kitchen for a few hours today. I'm scheduled to do that three times a week. That will get me out of the house."

"I never thought of you as the charitable sort."

"Because I'm too self-centered?"

"No, too worried about being patronizing."

"People have to eat. I simply dole it out to them—hopefully in an nonpatronizing way."

Andrea frowned. "Isn't there some new project you could find to work on? One that used more of your training and skills than handing out food does."

"You know that I've had trouble concentrating ever since Barbara died. I can still manage the easy things, like teaching, just not the hard, original stuff. A scholarly project just isn't in the cards."

"Maybe you could go visit Amy."

"Now that would be a project," Charles said with a smile.

"What I mean is that she might have some ideas for what you can do."

"I'm sure. But I'm afraid she'd never let me come back. She's already been talking about having me move to some place near Boston."

"I've never noticed that anyone, with the occasional exception of Barbara, has ever had much luck in forcing you to do much."

"But family members do exert more pressure than others. Can you imagine me as a fulltime babysitter for my grandchildren during the day and spending my evenings discussing the stock market with Philistine Jack?"

Andrea grinned. "That's an image I'll always cherish."

She stood up to go.

"Do you have to leave?"

"I'd better get back to work. Now that I'm actually teaching in my field of American literature, I'd better get going on that proposed book. I'm working on an article on *The Woman's American Home* by Catherine and Harriet Beecher Stow. It was the standard domestic handbook for women in the nineteenth century. If the article works out, I hope it can be a major chapter in my book."

She gave Charles a hug, then stepped back and looked at him.

"Try to be happy. I'll give you a call, and we can have lunch or dinner together in the next couple of weeks."

Charles watched her go down the walk, and thought that happiness was probably too much to expect.

Chapter Twelve

Charles was up bright and early the next morning to go running with Greg. His legs were still a little stiff from yesterday's run, so he touched his toes and did a couple of half-hearted deep knee bends to loosen up before going out the door to meet Greg. After exchanging a brief good morning, they began to run, and Charles was happy to find that he went six blocks further than yesterday before having to stop.

"I didn't think people ran everyday. Don't they take a day off in between?" he asked.

"Depends on how serious they are," Greg replied, running in place. "I take one day off a week. You can decide that for yourself once you're able to run a mile. If you start taking days off before you reach a mile, you're likely to quit. I'm just trying to get you over the hump."

"How much further is a mile than what I ran today?"

"A little more than twice as far."

"How long before I can do that?"

"Two or three more runs. You're coming along fast."

Charles considered the matter. "Okay. We'll do it your way."

"You're not having a lot of major aches and pains, are you?"

"No, just some minor ones."

"They'll work themselves out."

Charles nodded and waited for Greg to resume his run, so he could head home. But Greg stayed there running in place.

"Is there any more information on the Underwood killing?" he asked.

"Not really. The police are still investigating."

"You know that Underwood was going to get one of the Opal College Chairs."

"That's what the Dean told me."

Greg's mouth set in a hard line. Charles might have let it go, but then he remembered his decision to look into the Underwood murder. He would never gather any data if he did didn't ask questions.

"Was there some kind of a problem with that?" he asked.

"Well, the next one of those chairs was supposed to be given to someone in the sciences. I was in the running for it."

"I didn't know about that. Will you get it now that Underwood is dead?"

"Too soon to tell. The head of the science division has already protested to the Dean and Provost about the attempt to take it away from the sciences. I think we have a pretty good chance of getting it back. Whether I'll be the one to get it is still uncertain."

Charles recalled his last conversation with the Dean where he mentioned that using the Opal Chair to get another English person might be a problem. Now he could see why.

"But you have a good shot at it if the sciences get it back?"

Greg nodded. "I think so. My scientific papers and teaching are better than the other candidates."

"I guess it would be a nice position to have."

"You bet. You get every fourth semester off from teaching and a nice boost in salary. Plus there's the honor of having an endowed chair."

Greg's eyes lit up with more enthusiasm than Charles had ever seen. Ambition was apparently a larger component in his personality than Charles would ever have thought. He gave Greg a long look. He was tall, sinewy, and easily strong enough to kill someone with a blow to the head. Charles had always attributed Greg's lack of emotion to being in the sciences, but what if he was a sociopath? Even Ruth had mentioned that he had a hard time relating to people. But it was quite a leap from being a bit distant with others to being a murderer. Charles also had trouble imagining Ruth being married to a killer and not realizing it. Maybe she did, and it didn't bother her. Maybe she thought of it as just another of her husband's charming eccentricities. Charles frowned. That was pretty hard to believe.

"See you tomorrow morning," Greg said. Abruptly he turned and ran off at twice the pace he kept with Charles.

"He runs like an antelope," Charles said to himself as he watched Greg disappear into the distance. "Although maybe I should come up with a more predatory animal, a lion or hyena perhaps."

Chapter Thirteen

Later that morning, Charles stepped into the English Department Office. It was his first foray there since being found a person of interest, and he was wondering what the reaction of his colleagues and the staff would be. But the only college employee was Sheila, the undergraduate who took over when the regular secretary was away, and she was currently staring fearfully at a pregnant woman standing in the center of the office.

"Where is Garrison Underwood? I want to see him *now,*" the woman said loudly and angrily.

Looking like she was about to cry, Sheila gasped out, "He's dead."

"Don't give me that. I know he told you to say that, but I want the truth. Remember, I'm very pregnant and he's the father, so there's no telling what I might do. There's no point in lying to me."

The woman advanced toward Sheila as if threatening to either hit her or give birth in the middle of the office. Sheila saw Charles standing in the doorway, and shot him a pleading look.

"Tell her Professor Bentley."

Charles walked further into the office and the woman turned toward him. She would have been quite attractive if her face weren't mottled with patches of red and her mouth twisted into a sneer.

"Hello, I'm Charles Bentley," he said, putting out his hand.

Taken aback by politeness, she took his hand. "I'm Nora Chapman."

"I'm afraid that Garrison Underwood is indeed dead. I saw the body. Apparently he was murdered."

"So the bitch finally killed him," Nora announced.

"Which bitch?" Charles asked automatically, then realized he probably shouldn't have said that in front of a student.

"That damned Sylvia. The one he married, that toffee-nosed bitch. He sure wasn't getting much from her, that's why he came to me. Couldn't keep him off me with a stick."

"I see," Charles replied neutrally. "But why would Sylvia kill him?"

"For money, why else? She insisted that Garrison get a ton of life insurance as soon as they married. Plus she's his literary executor and heir. His book *Critical Theory and Literature* is standard college reading. She'll clean up on royalties alone."

Charles gave her a level stare but said nothing. Maybe Sylvia could kill Underwood out of excessive greed, but this woman could have killed him out of sheer hate.

"Where is she staying?" the woman asked Sheila, who seemed fascinated by the conversation and only stared in response.

"Wake up!" Nora shouted. "Do you know where Sylvia Underwood is staying?"

Sheila glanced at Charles, as if asking for permission to give out the information, but Charles merely shrugged. Being retired meant he didn't have to make such determinations anymore. Apparently arriving at a decision, Sheila snatched a piece of paper up from the desk and stared at it as if the words were unintelligible. Charles thought that to her addled mind they probably were.

"She's staying at the Northrup guest house."

"And just where might that be?" Nora asked.

"On the north end of the campus," Charles said, when Sheila stood mute. "It's within walking distance if you can manage it."

"Don't worry," she said, shooting him a fierce grin. "When it comes to Underwood I could walk across the Sahara pregnant with twins." She gave Charles an appraising look. "Would you be willing to accompany me?"

"Do you feel you might need help getting there?"

"It might be safer to have someone with me when I do get there."

"Are you afraid Sylvia will attack you?"

"No, just the opposite."

"Why do you want to see her?"

"I want to talk about the disposition of Garrison's estate. Don't worry, I'll try to keep it friendly."

Charles paused. "Okay, I'll go with you."

Five minutes later they were making their way across campus. Charles found he had to stride along to keep up with the woman whose rolling walk, like a sailor who had been at sea a long time, still managed to cover the distance swiftly.

"On your right is Opal Memorial Library, the oldest building on campus," he said, pointing to a stately building with Doric columns.

"And the cantilevered building on the left is the new fine arts center. An interesting structure, although some believe it doesn't fit with the overall look of the campus. And right in front of us at the end of the quadrangle—

"Enough. If I wanted the fifty cent tour, I would have paid for it," Nora said, picking up the pace.

Charles imagined that he could see the fetus marching along in front of her, anxious to confront the bitch who had killed its father. The *its* reminded Charles that he didn't know the gender of the child.

"Boy or girl?" he asked.

Nora gave him an irritated glance. Sweat was beading on her forehead and her breathing was raspy.

"What?" she asked in exasperation.

"I was just wondering about the sex of your child."

"A girl, thank God. At least I'm not bringing another faithless, irresponsible man into the world."

"Good thing," Charles muttered, not without irony.

Charles kept silent for a while, and soon they had reached the end of the quadrangle.

"I thought you said this was within walking distance. I should have hired a Sherpa."

"It right over there," Charles said, pointing to a white house on the corner of the next street. It was the last in a line of small cottages where the college put up temporary guests. Not having much beyond minimal decor, they made Charles think of KGB safe houses.

They finally turned up the walk to the front door. Charles was about to knock, but Nora turned the handle and marched right inside. I guess she wants the advantage of surprise, Charles thought.

Nora went down a short hall. Charles hurried to keep up with her in case Sylvia was waiting around a corner ready to pound on an intruder. Nora turned the corner into a room. She came to such an abrupt halt that Charles bumped into her, almost knocking her to her knees. She collapsed into him. He caught her under her arms and barely managed, given her front-heavy condition, to pull her back to her feet. When he had her righted, he looked up and saw what had caused her to stop short.

Sylvia Underwood was lying on her back in the center of the room. He arms were stretched out above her head as if she had topped over backwards while leading a cheer. Most of her white blouse had turned red.

Charles was about to suggest that Nora sit down on the sofa right inside the doorway, but then decided that the police might not appreciate their lounging around at the scene of a crime. Resting in direct view of the body also might not be very relaxing.

"Let's go back outside," he suggested softly, gripping Nora firmly by the shoulder.

Offering no resistance, she allowed herself to be led out to the front porch, where they sat down on two old side-by-side rockers. Nora appeared pale and confused. Charles wasn't sure whether she was disturbed by the sight of a murder victim or by having been beaten to the punch. He pulled out his phone and gave the police the necessary information.

When he was finished, he turned and studied Nora. Her blank stare had been replaced by a more calculating expression.

"Maybe this isn't so bad after all," she said slowly.

"In what way? Charles asked.

She simply shook her head and gave him a complacent smile. Although he tried to engage her in conversation, thinking it might be a good distraction from the horror inside, she refused to say anything more until the police arrived.

Chapter Fourteen

Lieutenant Thorndike put Charles and Nora in the back of her cruiser and took them to the police station. She had left a team of local officer and state forensics people combing through Northrup guesthouse. Charles wondered whether any one would ever stay there again. Being given accommodations in a place where someone had died violently would clearly put off some folks. Others, however, might feel differently. It might become the go-to place for campus visitors. Perhaps a ghost legend would grow up around it, providing a new addition to campus lore. Charles found he rather relished the idea of being involved in a piece of unsavory campus folklore. At least he wouldn't be completely forgotten.

When they arrived at the police station, the Lieutenant asked Charles to have a seat in the waiting room, and took Nora down the hall, probably, he surmised, to an interrogation room. He sat in an uncomfortable plastic chair and wished he had something to read, even one of the unsettling magazines about illness and disease that seemed so popular in doctor's waiting rooms. He guessed that the police figured a person of interest didn't need any distractions. Better to leave them alone to confront their guilty consciences.

Not for the first time, Charles thought about what a large role reading played in his grasp of reality. Even when he was doing other things, such as eating or relaxing, he usually had some form of print in front of his eyes, and his mind was focused there rather than on what was around him. Did people who couldn't read have a better handle on true reality because they weren't always escaping into an imagined world? Could the being in the present moment so talked about by meditators be easily achieved if people were kept illiterate?

Charles brooded on that for almost forty minutes, when Lieutenant Thorndike appeared in the doorway and told him to go down the hall to the first room on the right. He went into a small room with a table in the middle and four chairs. One wall had a large mirror and all four walls were painted pale green.

"Is that a two-way mirror?" Charles asked.

"Nope, that's in the other room. This one's here just so I can check how I look."

Charles gave her an inquiring glance, but she just smiled and motioned for him to sit down.

"Can you tell me in your own words what happened from the time you met Nora Chapman to the time you discovered the body of Sylvia Underwood?"

Charles presented the events, trying not to embellish.

"Did Chapman seem to be surprised to see Sylvia Underwood lying dead on the floor?"

Charles frowned. "Of course, she did. Who wouldn't? Unless . . . oh, I see your point. What if Nora had killed Sylvia earlier and gone looking for a alibi, so she comes to the English Department office to get someone to accompany her back to the scene of the crime and establish her innocence?"

"You're pretty good at this, Charles. Maybe you should be occupying my seat."

"But is that scenario likely?"

"It's possible. No one in the neighborhood of the guesthouse saw anything all morning. She could easily have left and come back with you as an audience for her surprised act."

Charles shook his head in disbelief. "Not unless she deserves to be in the running for an Academy Award. Nora seemed truly stunned at finding Sylvia dead."

"There was nothing suspicious about her behavior?"

"Well, she did seem to recover rather quickly, but she does seem to be a resourceful young woman. Her last words to me, however, were a bit strange," Charles said, and he repeated them to the Lieutenant.

"Not really that strange at all," Thorndike said. "Think about it. Garrison Underwood had no surviving family other than Sylvia. With Sylvia gone, Nora can make a plausible claim that her child will be Underwood's only surviving heir."

"And the estate should be sizeable," Charles said, and he reported what Nora had told him about the insurance and royalties. "But would Nora have told me all that if she had this scheme in mind."

"That's one flaw in the theory. A bigger one is that I've checked with the airlines, and Nora didn't get into Boston until late yesterday. There's no way she killed Garrison Underwood, and as I told you before, I find it hard to believe that we have two separate murderers in Opalsville."

"Maybe we should reconsider. She could have had a boyfriend or a paid associate kill Underwood."

Thorndike shrugged, unconvinced. "We're keeping her under surveillance, so if she meets up with anyone, we'll know. So stay away from her. She could be dangerous."

"She's not my type," Charles said.

"You mean pregnant."

"No, I mean scary."

Thorndike smiled.

"How was Sylvia killed?" he asked. "All I could see was a lot of blood, but I had no idea what caused it."

"She was shot. According to preliminary reports, she was shot right through the heart. It was clean and quick."

"Not like the person who shot at me."

"Could be the same individual if he was just fooling around with you to lead us astray."

"But how would Nora or an associate have known about me at all. It's got to be someone else."

The Lieutenant nodded. "Good point. Unless her associate was someone who knew the campus."

"And would the same person have killed Underwood by hitting him over the head have killed Sylvia with a gun. That seems like awfully inconsistent modus operandi."

"He's a murderer, not a logician, Charles. He might use whatever seems to work at the time."

"A pragmatist?" Charles asked.

"If you say so," the Lieutenant replied.

"It's seems to me that if the same person killed both Underwood and Sylvia. He wasn't sure about killing Underwood when he went to see him or he'd have brought his gun. But he was certain about the need to kill Sylvia. I wonder why the need to kill her?"

"When we know that, we'll be well on our way to solving the case."

Chapter Fifteen

As Charles headed out to the soup kitchen the next day, he admitted to himself that he was in an uneasy state of mind. He'd spent much of the morning trying to read the paper, but frequently found his thoughts drifting off to the two murders. As much as he tried, he couldn't picture Nora Chapman killing Sylvia with a gun. He could easily imagine her hitting Sylvia with the traditional blunt object in the rage of the moment, but calmly murdering her didn't match his view of the woman. There was also the problem of where she could have gotten a gun so quickly in a strange country?

She had only arrived in Boston that day, and even America, where guns were as common as dandelions in the spring, did not offer them to the uninitiated on every street corner. She'd have needed time and connections, both of which seemed lacking. He could more easily imagine her hitting Underwood over the head with the cricket trophy; however, she hadn't been in the country at the time. And the possibility he had discussed with Lieutenant Thornton of Nora of her having an accomplice, while it explained some things, still seemed pretty speculative.

That got Charles to thinking about who else might have gained by Underwood's death. It did seem as though Greg Wasserman had a better shot at an endowed chair now that Underwood had left the scene, but what would he have gained by killing Sylvia Underwood? He probably should have mentioned Greg's possible involvement to Thorndike yesterday, but it had slipped his mind. Probably selective forgetting because telling her would have made him feel like a snitch. But he decided to tell her at the next opportunity.

Finally, as much as he hated to admit it, he couldn't come up with a motive for Ernest Ritter to have killed Sylvia either. He clearly benefitted from Underwood's death, but not Sylvia's. Also, if Sylvia had had evidence that one of these men was guilty of killing her husband, she would surely have told the police, and not put her life at risk by remaining silent.

Charles pulled into the church parking lot and went down the stairs to the basement. This time John was waiting for him.

"About time you got here, Professor. These tables don't set themselves up, you know."

Charles ignored him and walked over to where the pile of tables was leaning against the wall. He took one end and waited until John did his jumpy little hippity-hop walk over and took the other end. Without speaking they worked their way down the basement, putting the tables into place. Soon enough they were down to the last one. Although John hadn't spoken, Charles sensed that the man was getting more and more agitated.

"You know, I don't like you much, Chuck," John whispered, coming to within arms reach and poking a finger in his direction.

Charles gave him a slow look. "The name is *Charles* and you can't imagine how little that means to me," he replied.

John's right arm went back, and although Charles hadn't been in a fight in his adult life, his time on the Amherst boxing team told him to expect a long right hook, the punch of most inexperienced brawlers. He ducked and John's arm went over his head. Ducking under it, Charles seized John's arm and pulled it up behind him while shoving his face into the basement wall. John gave a grunt of pain as Charles pulled his arm higher.

"Go ahead, break my arm, see if I care," the man hissed defiantly. "I can handle pain."

"Oh, I'm not going to break your arm, but if you try that again, I will tell Nancy that you tried to hit me. She'll fire you, and I suspect this job means something to you."

"And I'll say it never happened!"

"And which of us do you think she'll believe?"

The fight went out of the man like the deflating of a balloon. Charles figured that this job was about the only thing in his life that gave John a semblance of dignity, and he wouldn't want to risk losing it. Although not proud of getting into a physical altercation with this down-and-out guy, Charles did feel a sense of satisfaction that his point had been made with greater clarity than would have been possible with a lengthy exchange of ideas. The intellectuals approach to things was not always the most direct or effective.

He let go of John's arm. The man slid along the wall and walked away without looking back at him. How their relationship would develop in the future seemed up for grabs. It could make his working here more difficult. Charles walked over to the serving table, lost in thought over whether there was any way to make amends to John in a way that wouldn't insult him more.

"So you did come back!" a voice exclaimed in his ear.

Charles turned in surprise and saw Karen Melrose standing right next to him.

"Sorry to surprise you. I just couldn't believe you actually returned."

"I told you I would," Charles replied, slightly hurt that he'd been doubted.

"People say all sorts of things."

"I don't," Charles wanted to reply, but decided that sounded too pompous.

"I've got something for you," Karen said with an almost flirtatious smile as she motioned for him to follow her. Reluctantly, he walked behind her across the basement to the kitchen. She opened the refrigerator door and took out a large paper bag. Inside was a metal pan. She slowly lifted the aluminum foil covering it to show him a cake of some kind. Charles stared at it.

"You did say it was your favorite," she said accusingly, when he didn't respond. "It's a blueberry crunch."

"Of course it is," Charles said, smiling brightly. He vaguely remembered having at some point in yesterday's conversation having said he liked blueberry crunch.

Karen handed it to him. "It's for you."

"Why thank you," he said, forcing even high wattage into his smile.

"Now I'll leave it right here in the refrigerator, but don't forget to take it with you when you go."

"I won't forget," he promised.

He hurried back out to the serving line. Once again Karen got the spot right next to him. She told him more about her late husband, who had been an accountant, and bragged a bit about her son and daughter: one was a dentist and the other a lawyer. He couldn't remember which was which. Feeling a burning need for levity at any price, he almost asked her which one she thought inflicted more pain on people, but decided that, given Karen's sense of humor, such a comment would be poor payment for the blueberry crunch.

75

But he spent much of the time feeling trapped, as though the smiling, chatting, Karen Melrose was pulling him into her web one fine conversational strand at a time. For one crazy moment he even envied the men in the food line who, although poor and mostly homeless, were enviably free. When the lunch was over, and he had once again pushed the food around his plate leaving most of it unconsumed, he helped the now completely uncommunicative and sulking John put the tables away.

He was heading for the door to leave when Karen called across the length of the basement, "Now, don't forget your blueberry crunch."

Several of the other women, although they kept their faces toward their tasks, smiled. Charles had the sinking feeling that he and Karen were well on their way to becoming an *item*. As he walked across the room, carrying the bag in front of him, an obvious sign that he and Karen linked together by the bond of food, he thought that an invitation for her to come home with him and share a piece of crunch would have been quickly accepted. He admitted reluctantly to himself that the idea such companionship wasn't completely unpleasant, but he couldn't find the will to place the noose of a relationship around his own neck.

Chapter Sixteen

After his morning run with Greg, where Charles, to his delight, managed to eek out five more blocks than yesterday, he returned home, showered, and spent a leisurely hour over his breakfast, the newspaper, and coffee. When the phone rang, he was surprised to see by the German cuckoo clock on the kitchen wall that it was already nine-fifteen.

"This is Lois in Dean Caruthers office. Would you be able to come in to meet with the Dean at ten o'clock this morning?"

Although tempted to say that he couldn't fit it into his busy social schedule, Charles decided that would be childishly spiteful, so instead he agreed. He quickly got ready and enjoyed his brief ride through the Berkshire Hills where the light greens of spring were already beginning to darken into the deeper hues of summer. Living among the hills and valleys might incline one toward being insular and having a certain narrowness of aspiration compared, for example, to western landscapes where one could see to the distant horizon. But there was something comforting and reassuring about living on a more human scale. Perhaps your dreams were smaller, but they tended to avoid the megalomania of those with fewer natural boundaries.

When he walked up to the Dean's secretary's desk, she glanced up at him, and then did a double take. Her second look seemed to Charles to be somewhat flirtatious. Although half-believing he was imagining it, Charles wondered why she would suddenly take such an interest in him. It was true that when teaching he had worn a jacket and tie, one of the last holdouts on maintaining a faculty dress code, and now he was wearing a soft knit shirt with casual chinos. Did he suddenly appear more accessible, more masculine? He also remembered that Lois was divorced, and so she might be looking for an eligible partner. He returned her smile with a polite one of his own, unsure how much encouragement he wanted to give her. He also wondered if it was a sign of creeping senility that he thought every woman he met had designs on him.

Lois went into the Dean's office to announce him, and a second later she motioned for him to come in. She gave Charles yet another smile as he walked past, which he answered with a friendly nod.

"Good to see you again so soon," Caruthers said, meeting him in the middle of the large room and shaking his hand. He directed Charles to a seat, and then settled in right across from him.

"I could have told you this on the telephone, but I wanted it to be in person. The College has awarded you the title of professor emeritus."

The Dean looked at him expectantly.

Charles knew that everyone who taught at Opal College for at least twenty years and didn't retire under a cloud received emeritus status, so he found it hard to muster much excitement. But he did manage a smile. It also seemed to him that it had been granted very quickly.

"Thank you. Remind me of what the benefits are of being emeritus."

"Well," the Dean began as if they were almost too numerous to mention, then he paused as if trying to recall exactly what they were. "Of course, it allows you to officially say you are a professor emeritus which gives you a certain stature."

"Right. Anything else."

"You are entitled to use the College athletic facility for free."

Charles decided that might actually be valuable. In the winter, when running outdoors would be unpleasant, he could always run on the indoor track, if he didn't mind being observed by students.

"You are also entitled to office space on campus." A light bulb seemed to go off over the Dean's head and he smiled smarmily. "In fact we've decided that as a particular token of the school's appreciation, you will be allowed to continue using your old office. We're sure it has many memories for you."

And no one else will take it, Charles thought. A murder scene office would definitely go begging. Even if most academics didn't believe in ghosts, they did believe in prestige. Whoever took that office would be admitting they didn't deserve anything better.

"Thanks," he said politely.

The Dean stood and put out his hand again.

"Please let me know if there is anything I can do for you. And if you do take up research again, we would be happy to have you give a presentation on campus."

"That would be nice. One last thing, it seems to me my emeritus came rather fast. Was there a reason for that?"

Caruthers cleared his throat and looked a shade embarrassed.

"President Simpson felt it was the least we could do under the circumstances."

Charles nodded. The President of the college, an American historian, had always admired Charles' work. It was nice to know that he was appreciated on some level.

Charles left the office, gave Lois a last lingering smile, and headed back to his car. He still had all his stuff from the office in the trunk, boxed up exactly as Underwood had done it on that fateful day. He drove around to the English Building and, leaving the picture of Barbara on the seat so he wouldn't forget to have the glass replaced, he carried the box up the back stairs to his office. Since he had never turned in his key, it was easy to get inside.

He settled into his reliable old desk chair and sat for a moment waiting to see if the office felt any different to him after the traumatic event that had recently taken place there. After a few moments, he decided that the old place was the same as ever, and he wouldn't be bothered by the memory of finding Underwood's body behind this very desk. Charles was an agnostic on the question of whether places where violent events had occurred gave off particular vibrations. He'd never experienced any himself, but he kept an open mind on whether others who were more sensitive to such things might do so. One thing was certain; there wouldn't be any competition for this office. Maybe in the distant future a new hire unaware of its history could be suckered into taking it, but until then it was his as long as he wanted it. Although keeping an office seemed to go against his policy of making a clean break with his former employer, Charles liked the idea of having somewhere to go other than home. Who knows, he thought, maybe some day he'd even start writing again.

Charles slowly unpacked the box, returning everything to its accustomed place. Even the rubber snake he had confiscated over twenty years ago from the male student who had thought it would make him popular to terrorize the female students. His efforts among the women had met with little success, but for the sake of class discipline Charles had taken the snake, and there it had stayed in the front of the top middle drawer ever since. He had just put the last of his pens in the drawer when Andrea walked past and looked inside.

"Is this Charles Bentley I see or his doppelganger?" she asked, smiling.

"It's the man himself."

"I thought you didn't want anything more to do with the College."

"Well, they made me a professor emeritus and the office came along with it, so I figured why not?

"Congratulations. I suspected you'd get it, but there's always the possibility that some administrator you'd offended over the years would block it."

Andrea walked in the office and sat down in the chair on the other side of the desk.

"Here to work on your article?" Charles asked.

She nodded. "Better to work here than at home where I can always find a distraction. Some days I find I'd even rather clean house than write. But I guess crime has been keeping you busy lately. I hear you found another body."

Charles nodded somberly. "Sylvia Underwood. I seem to be the innocent bystander to every murder that happens."

"Do the police have any idea who killed her?"

" I don't think so, and I have eliminated several suspects."

"Oh, you're working with the police now."

"We consult occasionally, but I'm conducting my own investigation, purely armchair."

"And whom have you eliminated while sitting in your armchair?"

"Ernest Ritter."

"Why?"

"He may have had a motive to kill Garrison Underwood, but I couldn't think of any reason for him to murder Sylvia."

"Makes sense. I'm sure you hated to cross him off your list."

"Indeed. I also decided that Greg Wasserman may have had a motive to kill Garrison, but he too had no reason to kill Sylvia."

"How is Greg involved in this?" asked Andrea with a puzzled expression.

Charles explained about the Opal chair being given to English instead of science.

"Wow! To do something that drastic the Dean really must have been desperate to get Underwood to come here. The science division has to be furious."

"With Greg leading the way, I believe. But, as I said, he had nothing against Sylvia."

"What about Nora Chapman? Rumor has it that she was furious with both of them."

"She was certainly angry at Garrison for leaving England in an attempt to avoid responsibility for his soon-to-be-born daughter. I don't know if she was angry with Sylvia, but she probably thought that her child should inherit part of Garrison's estate. Now, with Sylvia dead, the child might well get all of it."

"That gives her a prize motive for murder," Andrea said.

"She's a good suspect for killing Sylvia, but not for Garrison."

Charles went on to tell her what he had learned from Lieutenant Thorndike about Nora's arrival being too late for her to have killed Garrison. He also presented the scenario that Nora had had an accomplice."

"I like the idea of a male accomplice. I saw Nora around campus yesterday. When she's not pregnant, she would be a very attractive woman. A lot of men might fall under her spell."

"I see you don't subscribe to the view that pregnancy makes every woman beautiful," Charles said.

Andrea shrugged. "There's beauty and there's beauty. I don't think a pregnant woman is all that sexually desirable to men. Once Nora has her figure back, that would be another story."

Andrea checked her watch. "I'd like to take you out to lunch and play Sherlock Holmes some more, but I have a commitment today." She stood up. "But I promise we'll get together soon."

"I'll look forward to that," he replied.

Charles watched her as she walked out the door. When he'd been on the faculty, they'd eaten together at least once a week, which hadn't happened since his retirement. Of course, that was only a couple of days ago. Maybe he was making much out of a little. Still, the thought occurred to him that, when he had been in a position as a senior faculty member to help Andrea, she had paid more attention to him. Now that he had been kicked to the curb, she seemed a shade less concerned with maintaining their friendship. He shook his head and decided that he was being ungenerous. People did get caught up in things, and Andrea was in the middle of writing an article that could be important to her career.

"Are you busy?" a woman said from his doorway.

He looked up and saw Nora Chapman standing there, hands on her back and her protuberant stomach entering before her without waiting for a reply.

"Please come in," Charles said unnecessarily, wondering if the woman was carrying a gun. It didn't seem such an odd thing to wonder about given recent events.

As she walked into the room, Charles decided she probably wasn't armed. The hands pressed to her back were most likely empty, and she didn't have a bag. He doubted she was in any condition to hit him over the head with something or use a knife.

"I just came by to pick up Garrison's stuff. I guess I'm the closest thing to a relative that he's got in this country at least."

"I'm afraid that Sylvia had already taken whatever he left in the office. I don't know where it would be now. You'll have to ask Lieutenant Thorndike."

Nora made a face. "I'd rather not deal with her. I have a feeling that Thorndike thinks I murdered Sylvia."

"You did seem pretty angry with her."

"Not angry exactly." Nora patted her stomach. "I just wanted to make sure that Daphne here was going to get her fair share of her father's estate. And even if I was angry, I've been angry with a lot of people, but I've never murdered anyone. The worst I would have done is shouted at her if she refused to recognize Daphne's just claims."

"I see."

"Maybe you could talk to the Lieutenant and get her to go easy on me."

"Why would I have any influence over what Lieutenant Thorndike thinks?"

"I saw the way she looked at you when she drove us to the police station. There was more than just police interest."

Charles felt his pulse rate go up and his mood lighten, but he tried to ignore it.

"I doubt that."

Nora shook her head. "I'm good at picking up on things like that. She's definitely got a personal interest in you."

"Well, even if she does, I'm certain she's not going to let me influence the conduct of her investigation."

Nora's face turned a blotchy red and her voice rose angrily. "It's silly to think that I could have killed Sylvia. I've never handled a gun and my life, and where in the world would I have gotten one in less than twelve hours in a foreign country."

"There are ways," Charles said vaguely, although secretly he agreed with her.

"And I certainly didn't murder Garrison. I wasn't even in the country when he was killed."

"You could have had an accomplice," Charles said. He regretted saying it as soon as the words left his mouth because he might have been giving away a line of thought Thorndike wanted to keep confidential.

"An accomplice! What do you think I am? The head of a criminal gang."

She struggled to her feet and stood there staring venomously at Charles for a moment.

"I've got a lawyer—an American lawyer—and I plan to get out of this god-awful country as soon as possible. And I will also see that little Daphne get what she is entitled to have."

Turning as quickly as she could in her awkward state, she waddled out of the office. Charles sat there for a moment looking at the spot where she had been. She was certainly a mercurial woman: calm and reasonable one moment, full of angry self-vindication the next. He could easily imagine her hitting Underwood over the head in a moment of anger. Perhaps he would recommend to Lieutenant Thorndike that she double check on whether Nora was actually on the later flight or whether there was any way she could have arrived sooner.

Charles heard a rumbling in his midsection and realized that he was hungry. Debating whether to go home or not for lunch, he finally decided to go to the faculty dining room. There wouldn't be many people there in the summer, but just possibly there might be someone he wanted to talk to. Closing and locking his desk, a security precaution he had consistently followed over the years and carefully locking his office door behind him, he headed toward the student center.

Chapter Seventeen

The faculty dining room at Opal College had the appearance of a German beer garden. Dark beamed ceilings and shelves of ornate beer mugs were evident everywhere. Since the mandatory state drinking age was twenty-one, alcohol was never served on campus, except on special faculty/staff occasions, and then it was wine rather than beer. Charles had wondered what had inspired the decorations when he first came to Opal. Reading a history of the college, authored by a faculty member who had taught at the college for fifty years and was already ancient when Charles arrived, had told him that one of college's late nineteenth century benefactors, William Dornmeister, had provided the funds for the student center. A man who had studied in Germany, he was enamored of all things German, and had designed the room to imitate the German drinking halls of his youth. The sober, mostly non-Germanic faculty of today seemed to tolerate the room or at least lacked the passion to have it changed.

Charles went down the cafeteria line selecting only a turkey on rye sandwich and a cup of coffee. Although several of the desserts looked good, he resisted tasking one, concerned about his caloric intake now that he was no longer working. The thought of becoming the typical senior citizen with a bulging belly, wearing shorts and a tight t-shirt, filled him with horror. Perhaps if his running program worked out, he would be able to allow himself some sweets. Life was always a matter of negotiating with yourself between what you wanted and what you should have, and Charles prided himself on having the discipline to do that wisely.

Standing at the door to the dining room with the tray in his hands, he surveyed the room. In the far corner was a table where six administrators sat. Not getting the full summer off like faculty, they seemed to revel in having the dining room pretty much to themselves. Charles knew that administrators usually felt like they were the core of the college because they made most of the important decisions and knew the inner workings of the bureaucracy, as opposed to the faculty whom they regarded as rather lazy part-time employees. Charles was about to sit by himself on the other side of the room when he felt a hand on his arm.

"Well, hello, Charles, fancy meeting you here," said Clive Bishop who taught French. "Shall we claim a table and provide at least soupçon of academic respectability to the room."

Charles smiled. "You choose."

Clive led them to a table just outside hearing distance of the administrators.

"This way they can strain without success to discover what we might be plotting," Clive whispered.

"My plotting days are over," Charles said, taking his sandwich and coffee off the tray and placing them on the table.

"Ah, yes, so I'd heard. Congratulations, I suppose."

"Yes, I'm not sure about that either. First I was pushed out the door. Then I was invited back in, and refused the invitation."

Clive asked for all the details, and Charles provided them.

"The Dean should be thankful that someone bashed in Underwood's head before he got the chance to teach," Clive offered.

"Why is that?"

"Well, he taught in this country once before. Did you know that?"

Charles nodded. "His wife, Sylvia, mentioned that he had taught in the U. S. about ten years ago. She said he went back home because in England he could make more of a splash."

"That may be the reason he gave her, but the direct cause of his leaving was that he got fired. He definitely left Yale under something of a dark cloud. I'm surprised the Dean wasn't aware of this."

Clive speared some of his salad and chewed ruminatively.

"You know Caruthers. His academic contacts, such as they are, incline more to the social science than the humanities," Charles said.

"Yes, he is rather insulated."

"What did Underwood get fired for doing?"

"The specifics were always left rather vague, but it involved inappropriate behavior with female students."

"He must have been a bit old to have had any appeal to the undergraduates," said Charles.

Clive shrugged. "He was in his middle thirties and in the last glow of youth at the time. I remember him as quite a handsome man.

As I recall, he thought his appeal was universal, extending across the spectrum from undergraduate to graduate students."

"I wonder if he made any long lasting enemies. Someone who would still bear a grudge ten years later."

"Probably most of the Yale English Department, a number of select administrators, and a swath of the female student population remember him with malice, but whether that would extend to murdering him I doubt. Maybe revenge is best served cold, but I believe most people murder because immediate circumstances impel them to do so. If someone was going to murder him because of his behavior at Yale, I think it would have happened at the time."

Charles nodded, but wasn't convinced. Some people, he thought, had to let an idea ripen before they could act on it. The hills of New England were rife with long simmering animosities that only years later burst into outright violence. The more he thought about it, the more he was inclined to think that a student would be more likely to bear a grudge. After all, they were the ones that Underwood had actually abused. This suggested that it might be worthwhile to see if anyone on the Opal College faculty had been students at Yale while Underwood was teaching there. That should be easy to discover and might yield some new suspects.

Chapter Eighteen

When Charles got home he decided that the best way to find out whether any of Opal's faculty had been at Yale was to go through the school's website and check out the standard information about each faculty member, which would include where they had gone to graduate school. It would involve making an educated guess about the age of a faculty member, but Charles has at least a passing acquaintance with everyone on the faculty. Their rank would also help determine their age. Anyone who had been studying at Yale ten years ago would be no more than an associate professor.

He had just settled in at the desk in his study when there came a knock at the front door. Charles went down the hall and impatiently pulled the door open.

"Hi Dad," his daughter Amy said with a nervous smile.

"Well, hello," Charles replied after a startled moment, surprised to see her there since she never came without calling first. "I didn't expect you." He stepped back to let her into the hallway.

"I just happened to be in the area and thought I'd drop by." She patted her short brown hair into place and gave him a hug.

"Why did you happen to be in the area?" Charles said, as they went into the living room and sat down.

"There was a show at the Clark Museum I wanted to see."

"Enough to come all the way out here by yourself. That's almost a seven hour round trip for the sake of art."

"Well, I also wanted to see you. I was a little worried about how you might be handling forced retirement."

"You wanted to see if I was hanging from the chandelier."

"That's not funny," Amy said. "You know I worry about you out here all by yourself without Mom."

"I know you do," Charles said soothingly. "But there's no reason to be concerned. In fact my retirement has gone from forced to voluntary.

Charles went on to give an account of his latest conversation with the Dean.

"Are you sure you don't want to go back to work?" Amy asked.

"Positive. It's time for me to move on to a new stage of life."

That sounded like a television sound bite and excessively optimistic, but he hoped Amy would at least partially believe it.

"Doing what?" she asked, skeptically.

"I'm not certain yet. New stages of life are not something to be rushed into."

Charles could tell she was going to press him on the subject, so he changed the subject in a way that would pull her off track.

"The criminal investigation of the Underwood murder is proceeding apace. But there's been another murder."

"My God!"

Charles went on to fill her in on the murder of Sylvia. He left out the fact that someone had tried to shoot him on the patio as being too alarming. He could see Amy physically dragging him back to Boston.

"So," he summed up. "None of this really involved me in any way. I just happened to be among the first to find the body in both cases. I was a sort of helpless first responder."

"Maybe you should stay in more," Amy muttered.

Charles shrugged. "The campus of Opal has always seemed safe enough until now."

There was another knock on the front door.

"I seem to be exceedingly popular," Charles said, standing.

"Make sure it's someone you know before opening the door," Amy warned.

Charles pulled back the sheer curtain and saw Karen Melrose standing on the front porch with a package in her hand. She saw him before he could let the curtain drop and gave a big smile. Short of being obviously rude, he had to open the door.

"Hello," Karen said with a sort of breathless nervousness. "I was making a Bundt cake and the recipe made two. I thought maybe you'd like one."

She thrust the bundle towards him like it was a baby he'd abandoned.

"How did you get my address?" Charles asked, not reaching out to take the cake.

"There are only two Bentleys in the book, and you're the only Charles," she said, still holding the cake out in front of her." Tears were starting to well in the back of her eyes.

"Thank you very much for the cake. It was very kind of you," Amy said, edging past her father in the doorway and taking the cake. "Would you like to come in? I'm Amy, Charles' daughter."

Karen stepped inside and Amy invited her to come back to the kitchen leaving Charles standing stock still next to the door. He heard the animated female voices coming from the rear of the house. There was something soothing about hearing female voices again. The house had been far too silent for the past three years. Yet he couldn't get past a certain paranoia with regard to a woman who would so blatantly pursue him. He knew he should go into the kitchen and join in the conversation. It was boorish not to do so, but by the time he'd made up his mind to enter the kitchen, Karen was coming down the hall toward him with Amy close behind.

"Thanks again for the cake. It was very thoughtful," Amy said. "Wasn't it Dad?"

"Very thoughtful," Charles repeated.

Karen gave him a valiant smile.

"Well, I'll see you tomorrow at the soup kitchen."

When Charles didn't respond right away, she gave him a second glance.

"Won't I?"

"Yes, of course. And thank you," Charles amended, speaking slowly as though he were learning a foreign language.

Once Karen had left, he turned to face Amy whose expression indicated that she was less than pleased.

"You were very rude to that woman," she said.

"I don't like being stalked. I hardly know her and she shows up at my door waving baked goods around. There's no privacy anymore."

"You make her sound like a psychopath. She's just a nice lady with a Bundt cake."

"That's how it works. Don't you understand? You know which zebra on the Serengeti becomes dinner—the slowest—and that's the one that's had too many high calorie desserts. Gain weight, get slow, and soon a lioness is pulling you down. Yesterday a blueberry crunch, today a Bundt cake, it's all part of the plan."

"And would it be so bad if you got pulled down?" Amy asked with a smile.

Charles stared at her in horror.

"After all, it's been three years since Mom died. Don't you think it's time to start dating again?"

He shrugged.

"Mom would certainly not want you to be alone for the rest of your life. And you're still a fairly attractive man, although a bit cranky and obsessive compulsive. Why don't you ask Karen out on a date and see where it leads?"

"I know where it will lead, deeper into the tangled web of relationships and commitments."

Amy paid no attention to him and looked over his shoulder into the distance.

"I kind of thought you and Andrea might get together after Mom died."

Although Charles' heart sang at the idea, he scoffed. "She's only in her thirties. Hardly any older than you."

"I didn't say it would be a good thing, only that you were always attracted to her."

Charles grunted. He knew Amy had never liked Andrea. He always suspected she was mildly jealous because Andrea had replaced her as a sort of surrogate daughter.

"And if you don't want all that blueberry crunch, Jack and I will be happy to eat it. It's one of his favorites."

Torn between two unpleasant alternatives of eating the crunch himself and making Jack, the Philistine, happy, Charles marched out into the kitchen and put the crunch in a plastic container, which he thrust at Amy.

"Are you sure you don't want to keep some?" she asked.

"Take it."

"Thanks. Since when have you been working in the soup kitchen?"

"Just recently. Ruth Wasserman, next door, talked me into it."

"I doubt anyone talked you into anything. Probably once you heard the idea, you really wanted to do it."

"Why would I want to?" Charles asked, genuinely curious.

"Because of your good Protestant ethic—a day without work is a day wasted."

"Don't be silly. I can be as lazy as the next fellow."

Amy laughed. "Only if the next fellow is as driven as you are."

Charles made no comment.

"Well, I guess I should be getting on to what I came out here to do."

"You've already done that. You've checked on me."

"I meant going to the art gallery."

"Yes, you'd better hurry if you plan to beat the rush hour traffic into Boston."

Amy hugged Charles and kissed him on the cheek.

"Please promise me you'll give some thought to what I said."

"About what?"

Amy sighed. "About dating again."

"I'll definitely give it some thought."

After Amy left, Charles went out to sit on the patio, thinking it might not be bad to die by one clean shot. At least it was better than being hunted down.

Chapter Nineteen

T he next morning he ran with Greg and when they reached a corner a few blocks further than he'd ever made it before, Greg stopped.

"This is the half-mile point," Greg said. "I would suggest that you trying running back home from here and see how far you get. You probably won't make it today, but you will in a couple more days. After that we can see about increasing your distance."

"How far do you run?" Charles asked.

"Three miles a day during the week and ten on Saturday. I take Sunday off to recuperate. But remember, I'm at least fifteen years younger than you," Greg said with a small smile. "You might not want to run as much."

Annoyed by the remark about his age, Charles promised himself he would keep running and extend his distance."

Giving Charles a brief wave, Greg set off on the rest of his run. Charles started running back towards home, and although he ran with a newfound determination to improve his endurance, he had to resort to walking before he was halfway back. He regretted that he wasn't still running atop speed when he got home and found Lieutenant Thorndike sitting on the front porch.

"Still sticking with it, I see," Thorndike said, standing as Charles came up the walk.

"Nothing great is accomplished without discipline," he replied, sounding sententious even to himself.

The Lieutenant smiled. "So I keep telling my men. I knocked on your door, and when no one answered I figured you were out running."

"Isn't it a bit early to be out disturbing the citizenry?"

"I figured that if you were asleep, you'd come to the door to tell me to get lost, and we could still have our little chat," she said, unperturbed.

Charles sat down on the top porch step and she sat beside him. It seemed oddly domestic to Charles, as if they were an old married couple watching the world go by. He felt himself relaxing into the scenario.

"What did you want to tell me?"

"It appears that Sylvia died from one shot to the heart."

"That's pretty impressive. Someone knew how to shoot."

Thorndike shrugged. "It isn't that hard to do at close range."

"Still, it shows that the killer had a cool head. Their hand didn't shake and the gun didn't jerk high."

"That's true."

"Is that why you came to see me? To tell me this."

"I just thought you'd want to know."

Charles thought that maybe Nora was right, and the Lieutenant was interested in him. She seemed to be taking every opportunity to see him, so she either thought he was far guiltier than he was or she liked his company. Charles hoped it was the later.

"I have some fresh coffee inside. Would you like some? Say yes, because there's a couple of things I'd like to tell you."

Thorndike nodded, and they went inside. Pretty soon they were settled around the kitchen table with mug of coffee in front of them.

"Would you like a piece of Bundt cake?" Charles asked.

"A little early for cake, isn't it?"

"Any time is right for dessert," Charles replied grandly.

"Sounds good to me."

Charles got the cake out of the refrigerator and cut off two large slices. For a while the two of them ate contentedly, neither one speaking.

"I haven't had breakfast yet. This hits the spot," the Lieutenant said. "Did you bake it?"

"No, a friend brought it around."

Thorndike looked like she wanted to ask who the friend was, but restrained herself.

"What did you want to tell me?" she asked.

"Well, first is a piece of information I found out a couple of days ago and should have told you last time we spoke."

Charles went on to tell her about Greg Wasserman and the Opal Chair.

"So this Wasserman had a reason to want Underwood dead?"

"That may be somewhat extreme. But he definitely had something to lose by Underwood being here."

"You're right. You should have told me sooner," she said with asperity. "Why did you conceal it?"

Charles picked up the last crumbs of cake with his fork and frowned.

"Greg's been kind to be in his own distant way by taking me running. And I would have felt like a snitch running to the police with something he sort of told me in confidence."

"In a murder case there's a narrow line between a snitch and a responsible citizen."

Charles shook his head sadly. "I know. I was wrong. I should have told you. But partly, too, it was because Greg volunteered the information to me as though it never occurred to him that it might make him look guilty of murder. If he were the murderer why would he even have mentioned it?"

"To make himself look innocent. We'll look into his exact whereabouts at the time of the murder. We know he was in the area because he was talking to you in the parking lot within the timeframe of the murder."

"The other item I wanted to discuss with you is based on the fact that Underwood taught in the States once before, about ten years ago at Yale."

"His wife Sylvia mentioned that to us."

"What she probably didn't tell you is that he was fired because of improper behavior with female students."

Thorndike rubbed her chin. "She did neglect to mention that."

"It's possible that Underwood never told her or made up some other reason. Or maybe she was just protecting her husband's memory."

"How did you find out?"

Charles told her about his conversation with Clive Bishop.

The Lieutenant took out her notebook and jotted down his name.

"We'll have a conversation with Professor Bishop, just to make sure there isn't anything he left out. I'll also get in touch with the New Haven police department to see if they have any record of charges being brought against Garrison Underwood."

"Probably Yale handled it in-house, but it's worth a try."

They sat and sipped their coffees in silence for a moment.

"I had another thought," Charles said.

Joanna raised an inquisitive eyebrow.

"I was going to do this today, even if I didn't see you. I was planning to go on the internet and check out the Opal College catalogue to see if any faculty were at Yale around the time Underwood was there."

Joanna pursed her lips. "You mean in case a former student from Yale who harbored a grudge against him was working here."

"I know it's kind of a long shot that someone would act on a grudge from ten years ago."

"I've seen stranger things happen. Why don't we engage in a little research right now?"

Charles nodded and led the Lieutenant from the kitchen across the hall into his study.

"So this is where all the magic happens?" she said, gazing at the book-lined walls.

"It used to, but not anymore."

"Why not?"

"I haven't been able to write much since my wife died. It's a problem of focus."

"Maybe you need someone to write for—a special reader."

Charles thought for a moment. "You could be right. She did read everything I wrote and commented on it. She wasn't an expert, but she was intelligent."

Charles turned on his computer. When the screen was up, he went to the Opal College catalog.

"The faculty are listed by department, so we'll have to go through all the departments. We won't be able to tell who might have been a student at Yale ten years ago, but we can find out if anyone teaching here got a degree from Yale."

"Sounds like a start," Thorndike said, pulling a chair over so she could look over his shoulder.

They went through the faculty. Charles wrote down the names of anyone who had gone to Yale. When he as done, he showed the list to Joanna.

"Only three. Not much quantity, let's hope there's quality."

Charles put a line through the top name on the list.

"Why are you crossing him out?"

"Ralph Condon in political science is in his early forties, and I know him pretty well. He was already teaching here ten years ago. In

96

fact, I was on the search committee that recommended him. He's also probably the wrong sex, unless Underwood swung both ways."

The lieutenant shrugged. "Hard to tell today."

"There's a Deborah Gould in biology," Charles said, pointing to the next name on the list. "She's only an assistant professor so she's probably in her late twenties or early thirties. That would be the right age, but I don't know how much contact someone in biology would have with an English professor."

"Maybe they met at a party."

"Possible. Yale is a pretty large school, but you don't know what the pattern of interaction might be. We'll definitely keep her on the list."

"This last person, Jessica Rhyser, is in the theatre arts. She might have something to do with an English teacher, right?"

"That might be a different departments, but definitely closer to the same field. She is the most likely candidate. I served on a committee with her once. She's a rather attractive young woman."

"Are you supposed to notice such things about your colleagues?" Thorndike said with a teasing smile.

"You can still notice a woman's looks, but nowadays you can't comment on them—at least not in public."

"So we have two people worth talking to," the Lieutenant said. "Would you be willing to speak to them first? You might get more out of them than I would."

Charles nodded. He was sorely tempted because of his commitment to find the killer. "What excuse could I give for prying into their past lives?"

"You could say that Underwood was murdered in your office and the police have been questioning you. So you're interested in finding out whatever you can about Underwood's background."

"That's sounds pretty weak."

"You'll be surprise how willing people are to talk about someone once they're dead."

Charles looked across his office at the shadows in the far corner. A part of him wanted to remain secluded here, cut off from contact with the outside world, so he could continue to think about the past and what his current life might have been.

"You could be a big help," Thorndike said, touching his arm.

97

"I guess I could call her at her office or get her home number from the Dean's office, and give her a ring at home."

"By all means give them a call and say how you are linked to the murder, but ask to talk to them in person. The eyes are the most important sense when it comes to judging whether a person is being truthful or not."

"I suppose that's true," he grudgingly admitted. "I guess I have nothing to lose. I'm not on the faculty anyway."

"That's the spirit."

"But I'm a bit surprised that you would want me to take such an active part in your investigation. Especially since I'm a person of interest in the investigation."

She paused. "You're not a person of interest anymore."

"What am I now?"

"Just an interesting person," she said with a small smile.

Charles nodded. "Glad to hear it."

Chapter Twenty

When Charles went to the soup kitchen later that day, his mind was still filled with his conversation with Thorndike. He reprimanded himself for being infatuated based upon such a short acquaintance. He thought that not having been involved in the dating game for such a long time left his emotions close to the surface, so he was susceptible to any kindness or expression of interest. But he changed his mind quickly when he walked across the cellar, blueberry crunch pan in hand, and thanked Karen. She provoked a feeling of emotional claustrophobia in him that came close to pure anxiety. Why did he respond so much differently to the Lieutenant's expression of interest? Maybe because she seemed less needy and used a lighter touch. Somehow Karen seemed to have read is mind because after saying that she had enjoyed meeting Amy, she paused.

"I'm sorry if I seemed to be coming on too strong the other day. I always do that with the men I meet who are single and seem nice."

Charles waved his hand casually and mumbled something indistinct. He felt embarrassed and hoped that somewhere in all that she would discern that he wasn't exactly angry.

"Maybe we could start out by just being friends?" she asked.

"Of course, that would be best," he agreed quickly

"We'll still be working with each other three times a week, so we can see what develops."

Charles managed to nod, but felt a sharp wave of concern sweep over him at the idea of anything developing. He didn't want to leave the soup kitchen, but perhaps he would have to in order to avoid this relationship.

After setting up the tables with John, who now remained completely silent, making it seem as if a pair of mechanical arms was lifting the other side of the table, Charles and Karen worked side-by-side in a comradely fashion. Over lunch she told him about her stint as a guide in an historic home in Opalsville. She was supposed to play an historical character, but tourists kept trying to force her out of character so frequently that she eventually quit and took on the soup kitchen.

"I feel that public service is an important part of any life, don't you?"

Before Charles could mull that over long enough to answer, she went on, "Of course, you do or you wouldn't be here."

Not completely sure of his position on serving the public, Charles merely smiled.

After leaving the soup kitchen, Charles went to his office at the college still wearing jeans and a knit shirt, the most casual attire he could recall ever wearing on campus. He looked up Jessica Rhyser's number in the school phone directory and called her office, only to get directed to voice mail. He needed her home phone or cell number. He decided that since it was such a nice day, he'd walk over to the Dean's office rather than just making a call.

Lois, the Dean's secretary, gave him a long look as he made his request for Rhyser's number. For a moment he thought she was going to refuse because he was no longer technically on the faculty. Then she smiled.

"You look different in jeans," she said.

"Sloppy," Charles said apologetically.

She shook her head. "I was going to say younger."

She gave him a slow once over and he wondered for the second time in as many days if she would go out with him if he asked. He had a feeling she would, but again he wondered whether this was something in which he wanted to get involved. Going out with anyone who worked at the College opened up a whole new set of possible issues.

"Thank you," he said when she wrote down the number and handed it to him.

"Any time," she said, flashing him a smile.

Charles walked down the hall and found a secluded alcove. Since it was summer, the normally busy hallway was empty, so he felt free to use his cell phone to call Rhyser.

"This is Charles Bentley," he said when she answered the phone. "I used to tech in the English department."

"Yes, Charles," a businesslike voice said.

"I don't know if you're aware of it or not, but Garrison Underwood was found dead in my office, and I'm sort of helping the police in their investigations. I believe you were at Yale around the same time Underwood taught there about ten years ago, and I was wondering if you knew him."

There was a prolonged silence. Charles thought Jessica might be about to question his authority to work with the police. It sounded weak even to him. Then he wondered if her failure to speak was based on the need to hide something about her relationship with Underwood. After what was probably only a few seconds, but seemed longer, she came back on the line.

"I knew him because he used to attend the theatre productions, and I acted in some of them. But I wouldn't say I knew him well."

"You may remember more than you think," Charles said. "Is there a time when we can get together to talk about him?"

"I'll be in my office in half an hour. Meet me there."

Charles said he would and tried to thank her, but she had already hung up.

Not having anything to do for a half hour, Charles walked back to the English building and went up to the department office. Sheila, the student assistant was sitting behind her computer, as usual she stared intently at the screen as if it were a window onto a reality she only dimly comprehended.

"Hi Professor Bentley," she called. "That was a really terrible thing that happened to Professor Underwood, wasn't it?"

"Depends on who you talk to," Charles was tempted to say. But he kept quiet because he didn't want to further confuse a student whose ethics were probably already overly subjective.

"Yes, a terrible thing," he mumbled, getting his mail from the faculty mailbox: promos for textbooks, ads for new teaching technologies, and a request to review a book. He happily deposited them all in the trashcan. Being retired can be very liberating, he thought.

"And then somebody murdered his wife. That makes it like a crime wave," Sheila continued.

"I'm not sure how many murders you need to make an official crime wave," Charles said. "But it certainly is shocking, especially in a town like Opalsville, which is usually pretty peaceful."

"You said it. It's positively boring here most of the time." Sheila returned to starting at the computer screen, and Charles quickly made his escape.

Once back in his office, he settled in behind his desk, waiting until it was time to journey upstairs to Jessica's office. He found his mind drifting from Sheila's comment about a crime wave to the Lieutenant. He realized that, although she didn't show it, Thorndike must be under considerable pressure to solve the two murders as quickly as possible. Charles resolved that he would do his amateur best to help her arrive at a solution, with that thought in mind, he walked down the hall and up the stairs to talk to Jessica Rhyser.

Chapter Twenty-One

The door was open to Jessica's office. She was sitting behind her desk, apparently engrossed in a book. Charles rapped on the doorframe, and she looked up.

"Oh, come right in, Charles." She carefully placed a slip of paper between the pages of her book and gestured to the chair in front of the desk.

Charles settled as comfortably as he could into the hard wooden chair and looked across the desk at Jessica. She looked to be quite short, only a couple of inches above five feet, and very petite. But he had attended a lecture she had given once on dramatization, and he recalled that she was very lithe and dynamic. So even though the large desk seemed to overpower her, making her look childlike, he warned himself not to underestimate her.

She, in turn, was examining him. A thin smile played across her lips.

"I think this is the first time I've seen you in casual clothes."

"Sorry, I came right over from working at the soup kitchen," he answered automatically.

"You've adjusted quickly to retirement, already into volunteering."

"You knew I'd retired."

"Things get around."

Charles shrugged. "Just giving volunterism a try."

"So you want to know about Garrison Underwood?"

"I thought that the more I knew about the man's past, the more likely I'd be to find out who killed him. And if I discovered his identity, the police would be less likely to consider me a suspect." He knew he was exaggerating his suspect status, but he hoped it would soften Jessica's heart to his endeavor.

"If he always acted the way he did during his time at Yale, knowing his past will probably provide you with a superabundance of suspects."

"What did he do?"

"Garrison was a real hound of the most predatory sort. He would start out using his charm as the great young man of letters, and try to flatter the woman into falling into bed with him. If that didn't work, he tried to evoke pity with the old line that his wife didn't understand him. This was even though they had just gotten married, and she was living right in New Haven with him. If his victim didn't buy that one, the gloves came off, and he would warn her that her grades might suffer if she didn't succumb to his charms."

"Did his approach work?"

"Maybe at first with a few of the weaker minded undergrads, but those of us in graduate school pretty much knew better. Before long the word had gotten around the English Department, and female students avoided being alone with him. Finally he tried it on with the wrong woman, and she secretly tape-recorded his threats. She brought it to her faculty adviser, and from there it went to the faculty ethics committee. Underwood resigned rather than be brought up on charges, even though he had two years to go on his contract."

"Would any of the women victimized by him have held a grudge?"

"Long enough to bash him over the head ten years later," she said with a smile. "I doubt it. That's a long time to hold such a big grudge. Most people would have moved on by now. I didn't know he had been hired here until after his was dead or I certainly would have gone to Yuri and Dean Caruthers to complain."

Charles thought about that. He knew faculty at the College who had held grudges for thirty years or more. He wondered whether the younger generation, along with their shorter attention span, also got over things quicker. That would be one benefit of the media age.

"Was there anyone special—someone who might have been abused longer or more intensely than the others?"

Jessica pursed her lips. "I did hear that there was one woman who became his virtual sex slave for quite some time, but I have no idea who it was."

"Why would a woman want to do that?"

"Speaking hypothetically, since it's never had any appeal for me, I would guess that she might have been into a daddy thing or enjoyed being humiliated."

Charles shook his head in wonder.

Jessica gave him the patronizing glance youth often assigns to age. "People are different, Charles. Sexual desire can be linked to all sort of unconventional behavior. Surely you're aware of that."

"Theoretically rather than practically."

She grinned. "I guess that's pretty much true of me as well."

Liking her better for her honesty, Charles continued, "Deborah Gould was at Yale the same time as you. Did you know her?"

"I didn't know her while I was there. People in theatre didn't mix much with the scientists. But we've become friends since we've been here. Being women of around the same age has brought us together. Opal College is still, well, you know . . ."

"Old and male. Yes, I'm aware of that."

"Anyway, as the only two women who were at Yale then, we get together to talk about the so-called good old days."

Charles smiled at the idea that a decade was a long time. It was a third of your life when you were thirty, but only a sixth when you hit sixty. It shrank in proportion like looking through the wrong end of a telescope.

"Did Deborah know Underwood?"

"I doubt it. Like I said, the scientists pretty much stick to their own."

"Do you know if she's around this summer?"

Jessica nodded. "We had lunch last week. She's involved in some big project that's keeping her on campus all summer. If she isn't in her office, she's probably in the biology lab."

Charles thanked her for her time and headed toward the door.

"Do the police really suspect you of killing Underwood?" she asked with an incredulous smile.

Charles turned back. "I'm a person of interest. Do you find that so hard to believe?"

"I just find it hard to imagine you killing anyone. You seem so gentle and proper, I guess."

"I have my rough edges," Charles said mysteriously, and left the office feeling unduly annoyed.

Chapter Twenty-Two

Charles walked across the left side of the quadrangle to the science building. In his many years at the College, he had been in the building only a handful of times but had always admired its Corinthian architecture. He went up the steps between the two front columns. In the front lobby was a surprisingly modern looking list of room assignments. He saw that Deborah Gould's office was on the third floor. When he made his way to her office, noting with satisfaction that a climb which would have made him out of breath a mere week ago was now an easy accomplishment since the start of his running program, he found the door locked. The Biology Department Office was only three doors down the hall. The secretary sitting behind the computer there told him the biology lab was one floor up.

He found the room and walked between several rows of tables until he spotted a woman at the end of the aisle staring into a microscope.

"Excuse me," he said.

Although he hadn't spoken loudly, the large room made his voice echo. The woman jumped, flung her hand out, and a glass slide skittered along the counter top in Charles' direction. He reached out and caught it just before it would have fallen to the floor.

"I'm sorry for startling you," Charles said, walking up to her and returning the slide.

She was a tall and thin with dark hair that reached down to the middle of her back. She smiled a little nervously as she took the slide from his hand.

"Who are you?" she asked a shade abruptly.

"I'm Charles Bentley. I teach English literature here," he said, deciding not to get into the whole retirement issue.

She smiled and a look of relief passed over her face.

"Sorry to sound so unfriendly, but I get skittish working in this building during the summer. Usually I'm pretty much alone, and I always imagine that just anyone could wander in."

"I'm sure you're also particularly nervous because there have been two violent deaths on campus recently."

Charles couldn't be sure but he thought her expression suddenly closed, shutting him out.

"Yes, I've heard about that. Fortunately, it has nothing to do with me."

"Actually, I'm here to ask you if you knew Garrison Underwood."

"He had just come on campus, hadn't he? I doubt that I would have met him."

"You're right, you wouldn't have had a chance to meet him here, but he taught at Yale when you were there. Did you by any chance know him?"

She paused and gave the question far too much thought. Charles even thought he saw her blush slightly.

"You know," she said, "now that I think about it, I believe I had him as a professor in my sophomore English class. It was only for one semester, so I had pretty much forgotten him."

Charles nodded. In his experience even after thirty years students rarely forgot their college professors for good or ill.

"What did you think of him?"

The woman smiled. "Being a teacher myself I don't like to be too hard on him, but he tended to rambled and went off on a lot of digressions about himself and his achievements. Basically he seemed a bit full of himself."

"I'd heard he could be quite charismatic."

"I recall that some of the girls—especially those who majored in English—were quite taken with him."

"Did you ever see him outside of class?" Charles asked.

She gave him a level stare.

"I mean about a paper or an exam grade," he hastily added.

"Not at all. I got an "A" without any difficulty. I've always done just as well in the humanities as I have in the sciences."

"I'm sure. I was talking to Jessica Rhyser a bit earlier. I gather the two of you get together some times to talk about the good old days."

Deborah made a face. "These are the good old days. Now I can pursue my own research and not have to work on some project my professor wants me to contribute to that will advance his career. But

Jessica and I do get together to share war stories, although we didn't know each other at Yale."

"I see. Jessica was saying that Underwood was forced out because of inappropriate behavior with his female students. Were you aware of that when you were at Yale?"

She shook her head. "We science people keep pretty much to ourselves."

"But that must have been the year you had him for a teacher. Weren't there any rumors?"

"I had his class in the fall semester. I remember hearing that he didn't show up to teach in the spring. I do vaguely remember something being said about his having been fired now that you mention it, but I never knew what it was all about."

Charles smiled faintly. "Yes, I can see how you might have forgotten the whole incident since you were in biology, and he taught literature."

She stared at him hard to see if he was being sarcastic, then she led up the slide in her hand. "If there's nothing else, I really should get back to this."

"Don't let me delay you. And thank you for your time."

As Charles walked back to the parking lot behind the English building, he tried to imagine Brenda Gould as Underwood's sex slave, but he had to admit that the whole concept of a sex slave was so contrary to his understanding that his imagination was overwhelmed. He had felt more sexual energy coming from Jessica Rhyser, but that may have said more about himself than about her. And neither Jessica nor Brenda struck his as women who would be in any rush to abase themselves. But maybe sexual slavery was a sort of guilty pleasure, like the literature professor who reads graphic novels, and it doesn't necessarily bleed over into the rest of the individual's personality. He was still thinking along these lines when he heard a voice call his name.

Chapter Twenty-Three

He turned to his left and watched as Andrea walked quickly toward him.

"I called three times. I thought you'd never hear me. Are you becoming a truly eccentric professor in your retirement?" she asked laughing.

"I was concentrating on something and was oblivious to the world around me."

"Is that wise?" Andrea asked, her face turning serious. "There might be somebody out there trying to kill you. Do you have any more information on who shot at you?"

Charles shook his head. "The police are pretty much convinced that was a diversion and that the murder had everything to do about Underwood and nothing to do about me."

"So it's just a coincidence that you happen to turn up wherever the bodies are? I heard about you finding Sylvia Underwood shortly after she was killed."

"I was just accompanying Nora Chapman. That's the woman who is supposedly carrying Underwood's child. She wanted to talk to Sylvia about child support, and that's how we found the body. Of course, now that Sylvia is dead and Underwood didn't have any family, I guess Nora's in a good position to get all of Underwood's money for her little unborn girl."

"That gives her quite a motive for murder," Andrea pointed out.

"Unfortunately, she was flying over the Atlantic at the time Underwood was done in, although it is possible she killed Sylvia."

"Under the circumstances I wouldn't have blamed her for killing Underwood. It takes a special man to leave his country just to avoid child support."

"Apparently Underwood made a habit of mistreating women. He had quite a record at Yale."

"What did he do there?" Andrea asked.

Charles told her about Underwood's predatory history at Yale. He went on to tell her about his conversations with Jessica Rhyser and Deborah Gould.

"Why did you talk to them?" she asked.

"Well, I got to thinking that maybe someone from those days still had a grudge against Underwood."

"Ten years is a long time to have a grudge."

"Yes, but if you were going to find yourself teaching at the same institution with him, you might not be happy about it."

Andrea nodded. "But it doesn't sound like Jessica or Deborah knew him that well back in the day."

"At least they don't admit to it. One of them could be lying."

"I suppose it's possible."

"I keep trying to think of some way to really find out what went on back then. I've got to dig deeper."

"Have you been doing anything else other than playing at detective?"

Hurt at her dismissive tone, Charles paused. "Well, I'm still working at the local soup kitchen."

"So you're staying with it."

I may be the Scrooge of Opalsville, but when I start something, I stick with it.

"If it's something you enjoy doing, I'm sure it's very worthwhile. It might even be better than teaching because at least you'll come into contact with people more your own age."

Charles frowned. "That seems to be the problem," he said, and went on to explain about Karen Melrose.

"She's probably just a lonely woman looking for a nice guy like yourself. Maybe she isn't the right one for you, but don't give up on love. I know what a wonderful person Barbara was, but somebody will come along who is wonderful in a different way. You just have to be open to it."

"I suppose you're right. Although sometimes I think that the right match is about as likely as winning the lottery."

Andrea smiled. "I'm sure your chances are better than that. Someone will come along."

Charles nodded, a bit disappointed that she didn't see herself as that someone. Then the thought came to him that he wasn't much different from Underwood who thought his appeal was universal. A few long honest minutes looking in the mirror would disabuse me of that, Charles thought.

"Well, I'll give you a call about that lunch," Andrea said, giving him a quick hug.

Charles nodded and watched as she walked to her car and pulled out of the lot. As he walked to his own car, he wondered what he was going to do about his personal life, and how he was going to find out more about Underwood's murder.

Chapter Twenty-Four

Later that afternoon, Charles was sitting on the back patio peacefully dozing. He would wake up occasionally, hear the buzzing on the insects and feel the heat of the unusually warm late June afternoon, then slowly drift back into a twilight state between sleep and wakefulness. Nothing was on his mind, although he had a slightly guilty feeling that what he was doing was sinfully lazy. It was almost with a sense of relief that he heard the front door bell ring, jarring him into complete wakefulness.

He opened the door to find Lieutenant Thorndike on the porch. He invited her inside. His offer of iced tea or a soft drink was refused, but she did accept a glass of ice water. When they were settled around the kitchen table, he looked at her expectantly.

"To what do I owe the pleasure of this visit?"

She smiled. "Just an update from your friendly police department. I wanted to let you know that Nora Chapman has an alibi for the hour before she showed up at the English Department Office yesterday, which is roughly when Sylvia Underwood was murdered."

"What sort of alibi?"

"She was in a local lawyer's office trying to find out how she could get a share of Underwood's estate for her unborn baby. The lawyer says she was in his office for over an hour, and he remembers the time very clearly because she spent most of it raging."

"Raging about what?"

"Garrison Underwood, Sylvia, the American legal system, and whatever else came to mind. Apparently she caused quite a scene. I'm afraid it pretty much let's her off the hook for shooting Sylvia."

Charles nodded. "Like I told you, I found it hard to imagine her shooting someone. She'd be more inclined to bash them over the head."

"Like what happened to Underwood."

"Yes, but there seems to be a possible wealth of folks who might have wanted to do that going back to his time at Yale."

"Did you talk to Jessica Rhyser and Deborah Gould?"

112

Charles filled the Lieutenant in on what he had discovered.

"So they both knew him," Thorndike said.

"Yes. But they both adamantly denied having any personal involvement with him."

"Did you believe them?"

"I'm not sure how good I am at telling when people are lying," Charles admitted.

"There's no scientific way to know for sure. Even the police, who are used to seeing lots of liars, get it wrong. Did either one of them act nervous?"

"Jessica seemed pretty composed. I think Deborah Gould considered telling me she didn't know him, but had second thoughts. If one of them had killed him, would they even admit to having known him?"

Thorndike shrugged. "Maybe, if they thought we might be able to find out the truth."

"Well, my money is on Gould because she acted the most suspiciously."

"People act suspiciously for all sorts of reasons, but I'll have a chat with both of them to see what I can find out. But what motive would either one of them have to kill him even if they had been involved with him."

"Revenge," Charles suggested. "They say it is a dish best served cold."

"But after ten years it would be frozen."

Charles stared across the kitchen for a long moment.

"You look like you've come up with something," Thorndike said.

" I was just thinking about something Jessica Rhyser said. She claimed that when push came to shove, Underwood would threaten to lower a student's grades if she didn't have sex with him. Since he had used extortion in the past, I was wondering if he was planning to use it again."

"I'd say most likely he was, but he didn't have any students yet."

"True. But what if he had already tried it on with his new colleagues that he had known at Yale."

"You think he had something on Rhyser or Gould that he was going to use to extort sex."

Charles shrugged. "It's a possibility."

113

"I'll see what I can find out when I talk to them. But they are probably not going to willing to give it away."

"Have you heard anything from the New Haven police?"

"I talked to a detective down there who checked their records. They had nothing on Garrison Underwood. I suppose Yale handled it as an academic matter, and none of the women filed a police report."

"Unfortunate, a little time in jail might have been good for Underwood. Instead he just got to move on to somewhere new and continue his bad behavior."

Thorndike stood up and stretched, suddenly Charles was aware that she was very much a woman.

"Well, he paid the price eventually," the Lieutenant said. She started to walk towards the door and Charles followed. "I'll let you know what I find out from Rhyser and Gould."

"Thanks for coming by and keeping me up to date."

She nodded. "Were you sitting out on the patio when I rang the bell?"

"Yes."

"Are you sure it's safe to do that?"

"I thought we'd decided that the killings had nothing to do with me."

"I know, but until we have this case wrapped up and know what's what, I'd be happier if you would play it safe. Will you do that?"

"I really don't think it's necessary, but I'll certainly accede to your wishes."

"Thanks, Charles." Joanna smiled and touched him on the arm. "I'd hate to lose you so soon after we've met."

"Me, too," Charles said, tongue-tied by the moment of intimacy.

Charles watched the police car back down his driveway, then he went into his study and booted up his computer. He had an idea of what to do next in the investigation.

Chapter Twenty-Five

Charles carefully scrolled through the names of the members of the Yale English Department. Many of the full professors were people he knew, either personally from conferences or by reputation. But he doubted whether he could convince any of them to do what he wanted. He needed someone with whom he had a more intimate connection. Finally he found a familiar name among the ranks of assistant professors.

Adam Sussman had been one of the best students Charles' had ever had. Charles had been his mentor on his senior honors thesis, and had written him an excellent letter of recommendation to graduate school. He had gone on to Harvard. Charles had lost track on him after that, but apparently he had found an entry position at Yale. Most importantly he had thought so much of Charles and had such a fun-loving nature that it might make him a good candidate for what Charles had in mind.

He called the number for Adam's office and was delighted to find him there. After some initial surprise at hearing from Charles after all these years, the two were soon engaged in fond reminiscence over Adam's time at Opal College. When there was an appropriate pause in the conversation, Charles got down to the matters at hand.

"I don't know if the story has made its way down to New Haven yet, but Garrison Underwood was murdered up here a few days ago."

"Garrison Underwood! Of course I've heard of him, but I didn't even know he was in the country. How did it happen?"

"No one knows yet, but it happened in my office."

"My God! How horrible for you. I take it you weren't there at the time."

"No, I had just left to go out to the parking lot. He was going to be using my office while I was . . . away." Charles didn't want to explain his retirement.

"I see."

"Yes, and it is part of the reason why I'm calling you."

"Only part?" he asked shrewdly

Charles chuckled to hide his embarrassment.

"To be honest Adam, I have thought about you many times over the years. You were one of my best students. I'm afraid I haven't been very good at keeping in touch over recent years."

There was a pause. "I heard about your wife dying. I'm sorry. I'm sure that's made things difficult for you. And it certainly is great to hear from you now. What is it you want me to do?"

"Well, the police, at first at least, suspected that I might be involved in Underwood's murder because it happened in my office. They've gotten away from that's idea recently, but I'd still like to find out who killed him in case the suspicion comes back in my direction."

"How can I help you with that?"

Charles went on to explain about Underwood's problems at Yale ten years ago. When he was done Adam whistled.

"You know, the one time I heard Underwood speak at a conference, I thought he was one of the most arrogant bastard I'd ever run across. One of those guys who goes through life thinking he's entitled. So I'm not surprised that he'd be involved in something like this."

"Do you think it would be possible to find out some of the specifics of what he did? Maybe get names of the students involved. I'd particularly like to find out who this so-called sex slave was."

"Of course most of the senior faculty would have been here a decade ago. But getting them to name names might be hard. Some of them won't be willing to talk about anything that reflects badly on the institution, and there are others who, even if willing, can't even remember the names of the student they taught last semester, let alone students involved in a decade-old scandal."

"I realize that. But every department in every school has a sort of unofficial historian who is willing to share past gossip with anyone who shows some interest. I thought you might know someone like that."

"There is a fellow in eighteenth century poetry, Christian Geller, who occupies that role here. He' a thirty-year man, and thinks every events that's occurred on campus in that time is worth of rehashing, especially after he has a few drinks."

"Do you know him well enough to take him out to dinner and ply him with alcohol?"

"We get along pretty well. He's a bachelor, and I'm sure things get pretty slow for him during the summer break. I'll give him a call and set it up. Actually, it's been awhile since I've had a chat with the old boy, it might be fun. Plus I kind of like the idea of solving a mystery. That's what scholarship is really all about, isn't it?"

"You're absolutely right."

"So we both should be really good at this sort of thing."

Charles smiled at the enthusiasm coming down the phone line.

"Indeed we should, Adam, indeed we should."

After he hung up the phone, Charles sat at his desk lost in thought for a moment. He had greatly exaggerated to Adam the threat he felt from the police. He doubted very much that suspicion would ever again fall on him, especially now that the Lieutenant had made him virtually a participant in the investigation. So why was he so anxious to discover who had killed the egregious Underwood, a man, who to all accounts, deserved to be murdered more than most. It wasn't because in principle he believed that all killers must be brought to justice. His ethics were much more situational than that, and he could easily imagine hoping that someone who assassinated an evil dictator got away scot-free. So why this determination to hunt down a killer who might well be someone grievously wronged by Underwood in the past?

Part of it, he knew was because Sylvia Underwood had been murdered. Finding her body still haunted him. He had liked her during their one brief meeting, and she had certainly suffered at the hands of Underwood as much as anyone. There was nothing from her past that indicated that she deserved to die. Since he suspected that the same person had killed twice, he believed that finding Underwood's killer would also reveal Sylvia's. She deserved justice.

But there was more to it than that. Since his involvement in the Underwood case, he had thought less about his past with Barbara. Less about the question of why she had been out on that snowy road late at night. Her death had stopped being the default setting that his mind drifted to when not engaged in immediate matters. For the first time in three years something had caught his interest. He leaned back in his chair and listened to its familiar squeak. Adam had been right. Some of the skills similar to those required in scholarship applied to the investigation of crime, but solving crimes, because they involved injuries to people, were unlike scholarship in that they were never trivial. Perhaps by engaging with something important, he could get on with his life.

He walked from his study and turned down the hall. For a moment he imagined that he heard the soft voices of Barbara and Andrea as they talked while working in the kitchen during the many times Andrea was over to dinner. The comforting sounds of the women still gripped his heart, but some of the sharp longing for the past had disappeared.

Chapter Twenty-Six

Charles ran again the next morning with Greg Wasserman, and this time when he turned around at the half-mile point and headed back to his house, he made it to within a block from home before he had to slow to a walk. Tomorrow for sure, he promised himself, he'd finally be able to run a mile. The thought brought an image to his mind of himself and Greg running off to meet the horizon, covering great distances with the speed of antelopes. How much can a man of your age reasonably be expected to do? The questioned suddenly loomed up puncturing his swelling balloon of excitement. Well, I guess I'm about to find out, he told himself defiantly.

After having breakfast, Charles decided to go into the College. He thought that another way to discover who had killed Underwood, assuming it was someone from his past, would be to find out if he had shown a special interest in any member of the faculty. Yuri, the department chair, had spent more time with him during his brief sojourn on campus than anyone else, so a conversation with him might be beneficial. Conversations with Yuri were always a shade surrealistic, but sorting out the impressions from the facts might yield some valuable evidence.

Charles enjoyed the ride into the campus. It took him around narrow twisty roads that went dangerously near the edges of the hills, but what was a nail-biting adventure during the snowy and icy weather of winter was a bucolic treasure in the summer. Between almost running a mile and having a sylvan experience riding in, Charles felt so happily mellow that he went up the main staircase of the English building for a change. The faculty secretary, Martha Reynolds, was back at her usual post and asked how he was doing.

Since she had been out on vacation for the past two weeks, he had to spend some time filling her in on his retirement and the murders of the Underwoods. She told him about her vacation, which apparently involved a cruise through the eastern Caribbean.

"You look like you've lost some weight," she finally said, after running out of vacation stories.

"Well, it's been a difficult week. Plus I've taken up running with Greg Wasserman in physics every morning. Do you know him?"

"I don't believe I've ever met him, but I just heard his name recently." She frowned and stared across the room. "That's right, Sheila told me he was here a few days ago." Martha lowered her voice, "Apparently he and Yuri got into quite an argument."

"What day was this?" Charles asked.

"It was the day Garrison Underwood was killed. Sheila only told me about the argument yesterday because Professor Underwood's death had pushed it out of her mind."

Charles' mind raced. What if Greg had spoken to Yuri about the English Department's sneaky maneuvering to get the next Opal Chair for Garrison Underwood? Charles could easily imagine such a conversation degenerating into a rancorous argument. And what if Greg, after his unsuccessful meeting with Yuri, had foolishly decided to plead his case directly to Underwood. To do so he might have headed down the hall to Charles office right after Charles had left.

He could imagine the kind of greeting Greg's request for science to get the Opal Chair would receive from Underwood. Any appeal Greg might make to merit, justice, or equality would have been met with scorn. When Underwood had finally turned his back on Greg as a last sign of contempt, Charles could easily imagine Greg picking up the cricket trophy and dispatching this aggravating impediment to his future success. That would explain why he had met Greg when he did in the parking lot by the English building.

Charles paused. Greg had seemed awfully calm at the time for someone who had just undergone a burst of murderous frenzy. But who knew about people in science. Some of them seemed to Charles to be absolutely nerveless or perhaps it was their tendency to optimism about the fruits of science that kept them calm, for example only seeing atomic energy as a force for good. For a moment, Charles was tempted to leave the office and seek out Greg to find out what had happened that day. But then he realized that he might lay some valuable groundwork by pumping Yuri for the details of their conversation. He decided to wait to confront Greg until their run the next morning.

"Would Yuri be available for a few minutes?" Charles asked.

Martha picked up the phone to ask Yuri. He must have said yes because Martha nodded for Charles to go in. Yuri has his door open before Charles reached it.

"Charles, my old friend, how is retirement treating you?" Yuri asked, giving him a comradely clap on the shoulder.

"It hasn't been long enough to know," Charles replied somberly, not having forgotten Yuri's role in attempting to get him replaced with Garrison Underwood.

He went into Yuri's office, which had bookshelves on every wall and piles of book on just about every flat surface.

"May I?" Charles asked, pointing to the books on the only chair other than Yuri's.

"Put them wherever," Yuri said with an expansive swing of his arm, as if Charles should fling them about the room.

Charles piled them neatly on the floor next to the chair.

He sat down and looked at Yuri, who smiled at him with nervous expectation. Probably still having some residual guilt over the trick he tried to put over on me, Charles thought.

"I'm here to try to learn a bit more about Garrison Underwood. I'm helping the police with their investigations."

Yuri's face went still, an impassive mask. As Charles expected, mentioning the police had a dramatic effect on someone who grew up in the Soviet Union.

"But I know nothing about his death," Yuri protested. "I hardly knew the man."

Charles smiled reassuringly. "I know you had nothing to do with his death. But you must have gotten some sense of the man. Didn't you have some conversations with him?"

Yuri thought carefully as if checking the conversational terrain for landmines.

"We talked briefly on the phone a couple of times when he was still in England, and I picked him up at the airport and transported him here."

"That's over a three hour trip, surely you must have talked about something."

Yuri frowned. "He was convinced that studying British literature after nineteen hundred was a waste of time."

"Did he realize that was your field?"

121

"Yes, I told him. He called it the stinking effluvia of a corrupt culture."

"Did you talk about anything else?"

"He was quite expansive on the subject," Yuri said dryly. "It took up a great deal of time."

"Did he mention anyone on the faculty by name?"

Yuri nodded. "He mentioned you."

"What did he say?"

"He said that's you were quite good—a decade ago," Yuri said, sounding apologetic. "He also said that it was a good thing you were being put out into the fields."

Charles pondered that for a moment. "You mean out to pasture."

Yuri looked at the little notebook on his desk, but didn't reach out for it.

"Underwood was not a man who pushed his punches."

"You mean pulled his punches."

Yuri shrugged, his lack of concern a sign that he was extremely uncomfortable.

"Did he mention anyone else on the faculty by name?"

"No."

"Is there anything else about your conversation with him that was noteworthy?"

"There was one thing. I asked him why he wanted to come to Opalsville, which is pretty remote spot compared to London. He said it was a combination of business and pleasure. When I asked him what he meant, he didn't answer. I guess he was a real tight-hipped sort of guy."

"You mean tight-lipped," Charles corrected.

Yuri pressed his lips together to form a straight line and nodded.

"I heard that you had a conversation Greg Wasserman on the day Underwood was killed. Was it about taking the Opal Chair away from the science department?"

Yuri lips remained pressed together and for a moment Charles thought he wasn't going to answer.

"Yes. He came to accuse me of stealing the chair from science. I explained to him that it was all Dean Caruthers' doing, and he should see him if he wanted to complain. He was very angry with me and some harsh words were exchanged. He wanted me to refuse the chair and cancel the appointment of Underwood, and I told him it was too late. Underwood was already here."

"Did you happen to tell him that Underwood was down in my office?"

Yuri frowned. "I may have. I was quite overwrought and can't remember exactly what I said."

"Did Wasserman say where he was going when he left here?"

"I believe he was going back to the Science Department office. He wanted the science faculty to file a formal protest."

"But you didn't actually see where he went after he left your office?"

"No, I was simply happy that he had struck the road."

"Hit the road," Charles said.

"Yes," Yuri said, "that as well. Do you think Wasserman could have bumped on Underwood?"

"You mean 'bumped off.' What do you think?"

"He very angry when he left, but I think he is essentially a nonviolent man."

"I think so as well."

"But even nonviolent men . . ."

"Can turn violent under the right circumstances?"

Yuri gave a large shrug that seemed to embody all the unpredictability of the world.

Charles nodded his agreement.

Chapter Twenty-Seven

Wasserman could easily have gone right down to my office and confronted Underwood, and such a confrontation could just as easily have ended in violence, Charles thought, as he drove home. Even though Wasserman seemed a rather buttoned-up kind of guy when it came to his emotions, Charles could easily imagine that, once released, his passions would be quite explosive. He also thought that Greg was probably not a very good liar, most scientists in his experience were not, except in their professional publications where they had a reputation of exaggerating their findings.

Charles was starting to preview in his mind the conversation he would have tomorrow morning with Greg Wasserman when he became aware of an odd sound coming from the passengers seat next to him. He listened carefully. It was faint brushing noise as if someone were rubbing something bristly along the underside of the seat. Charles listened carefully, but the sound seemed to have disappeared. Still he felt more than sensed that something was in the car with him.

As he looked over at the seat next to him, taking his eyes off a treacherous stretch of road, he saw whiskers appear above the seat on the other side, followed by a nose, and then a pair of beady red eyes. Soon the largest white rat he had ever seen was struggling to pull its fat body up from between the seat and the door.

"Ugh!" Charles exclaimed, struggling to release his seat belt. After much fumbling it finally came undone, and he turned to slam his back into the driver's door. By now the rat had waddled over to the middle of the seat, revealing it's long pink tail, as thick at its base as Charles' thumb. It filled him with revulsion. The rat came to the edge of the passenger seat and raised its nose to sniff the air. Charles was sure that at any moment it was going to leap over into his lap. He could feel the sharp little toes walking around his lap.

Slamming his foot on the break as best he could from his awkward angle, Charles pulled in on the door handle and tumbled backwards out onto the road. He twisted as he fell, so the side of his left leg took the brunt of the fall. He looked up quickly, in time to watch his car proceed slowly down a fortunately gentle grade until it settled with an ugly thump against the metal guardrail.

Charles lay there is the road for a minute assessing his condition. Aside from the start of a throbbing in his leg where it had been in contact with the concrete, he felt okay. He hadn't hit his head or landed on his back. Suddenly aware that he was lying in the middle of the road, he climbed to his feet and did a little shuffling dance to see if his legs worked. They were a bit stiff, but nothing seemed to be broken. His left pants leg was torn from the knee down to the calf, but aside from a few superficial scrapes, the skin seemed to be intact. He started to walk slowly towards his car.

He stopped. The door had closed as the car rolled away, so probably the rat was still inside. Although getting back in the car and driving away would be the least complicated way of handling the incident, he couldn't bring himself to share space with the giant rat of Sumatra. Reluctantly he took out his phone and dialed 9-1-1.

"Hello. What is you emergency?"

"There's a rat in my car."

"Did you say a rattle in your car?"

"No. A rat. As in a large rodent."

There was silence. Charles suspected she had pressed the mute button so she could share the joke with a colleague.

"Where are you located?"

Charles told her.

"We'll have a squad car out there shortly."

Charles thanked her, then walked over and leaned against the guardrail. In a few minutes his leg began to sting, and he wished he had some cool water to wash it off with. Finally two patrol cars arrived. The two officers walked up to him together, keeping suspicious eyes on him as if he a man afraid of rats might be capable of just about anything.

"Did you have an accident?" the taller one asked after getting his name.

"There was a rat in my car. I jumped out and the car rolled into the guardrail."

"Is the rat still in the car, sir?" the shorter one asked.

"As far as I know."

He walked toward the car.

"Walt is good with animals," his partner informed Charles.

The officer opened the car door and climbed inside. A few second later he emerged carrying the rat in one hand, while he gently petted its fur with the other.

"This is no sewer rat," he announced as he walked towards Charles. "This is someone's pampered pet or a lab animal."

"How did it get in your car?' the tall officer asked, as if suspecting theft.

"I have no idea. I imagine someone put it there."

The cop smirked. "Why would anyone do that?"

"Because someone knew I have a pathological fear of rats, and they were hoping that if one appeared in my car during my drive home, I'd panic and go over one of these cliffs in a ball of fire."

The smirker laughed. "Now why would anyone want to do that?"

"This is the second attempt on my life this week. If you want details, call Lieutenant Thorndike of the Opalsville Police."

The smirker stopped smirking and his expression turned serious.

"Do you need some medical care for that leg?" his partner asked, coming closer than Charles liked with the rat.

"No, I'll be fine. Thanks for taking the rat out of my car. Can I go now?"

"Don't see why not? We'll just wait to make sure your car drives okay," the taller one said.

Charles walked around to the front of his car to survey the damage, which didn't look much worse than a dent in his bumper. He knew that to have it fixed they'd probably have to remove the entire front bumper of his car, and it would cost a fortune. Now that I'm retired, he thought, riding around with a few dings is almost a badge of honor. He got in his car and without difficulty drove the rest of the way home.

• • • •

TWO HOURS LATER, CHARLES sat in the living room with his leg up on a hassock. He had first thought about going out on the patio, but then decided one attempt on his life was enough for a day. He had put antiseptic on his scratches, which were annoying rather than severe. His leg ached a bit and had stiffened up as he sat, but occasionally flexing seemed to help.

Reflecting on what had happened, Charles realized that if the rat had appeared a few minutes later when the twists in the road were less forgiving and the downhill grade was more severe, this could easily have had a more tragic outcome. If his car had gone over the edge into the valley below, it was doubtful that anyone would ever have figured out what had caused the accident, and it would probably have been written off as the result of driver inattentiveness or of a stoke or cardiac event. Able to ponder the episode as a thing in the past, he could find enough distance to appreciate the brilliance of the idea. Someone had planned this out very carefully to make a murder appear as an accident.. The front doorbell rang and he sprang to his feet only to fall back and grab the chair as his leg refused to respond quickly. After straightening it several times, he was able to hobble to the door.

"How are you feeling?" Lieutenant Thorndike asked from the doorway.

Charles stepped back awkwardly to let her come inside.

"Looks like you've got a problem with that leg," she observed.

"I fell on it when I jumped from the car. I'll be fine with a little rest."

"Are you sure? I can take you in to the emergency room. I can even get you moved to the front of the line if I identify you as a suspected criminal we want to put behind bars."

"No, thanks. I think I'm already on the road to recovery."

"Seriously, maybe you should get an x-ray."

Charles shook his head. "I'll see how it is in a day or two."

They walked into the living room and sat down.

"So you were driving along and this big, white rat popped up from under the passenger's seat?"

He nodded.

"Well, I've managed to find out its name."

Charles stared at her hard to see if she was joking. "It has a name."

"I figured that it was put in your car while it was parked in the Opal College lot, so I called over to the science department to ask where someone would get a white rat on campus. They directed me to the experimental psychology lab. I gave them a call and, sure enough, one of their rats was missing. His name is Freud. Believe it or not, he shared cage space with Jung. I guess the experimental psych folks don't have a high opinion of psychoanalysts. One of my officers is taking Freud over there now. Apparently they were very worried about him because he's one of their smartest rats."

"You couldn't prove it by me," Charles muttered.

"But then you aren't a rat lover, according to the officers on the scene. Why this phobia about rats?"

"You mean you wouldn't panic if one turned up in your cruiser?"

"Maybe a big nasty gray ally rat would bother me, but not a lab rat. At least not enough for me to crash my car."

"It's a long story."

Thorndike made an exaggerated gesture of settling into the sofa. "I've got nothing but time. Crime appears to have taken day off except for your event."

Charles sighed. "I saw a lot of rats in Vietnam. *Ratus ratus*, the black rat, a little smaller than the ones we have here. One night I woke up in my hooch with a sharp pain in my big toe and there was one of them with his teeth in me, hanging on for dear life. I finally shook it free, and it ran off under the door."

Thorndike gave a little shiver. "That must have been terrible."

"That wasn't the worst of it. I made the mistake of telling my first sergeant and he told the medics. They insisted that I have a full round of rabies injections, that's twenty-one shots into the stomach with a long needle."

"My God!"

"Yeah, it was quite an ordeal. Three months later the Army decided that since no one in Vietnam had ever gotten rabies from a rat bite, the shots weren't necessary. Too late for me. So you can see that I have a bad reaction to rats."

"How many people at Opal College would know this story?"

"No one. I never talk about it. Even Barbara didn't know."

"Then why would someone know to put a rat in your car."

"Because two years ago I was eating lunch in my office, and I had to go out for a few minutes. When I got back, there was a big gray rat on my desk eating my sandwich. I ran out into the hall and made quite a commotion. Anyone in the English department would know my feelings about rats. Heck, it probably spread around the entire school. It's just the sort of delightful story that would make the rounds."

"So we can't narrow it down to a few people?"

Charles shook his head. "But I thought we had decided that the killer wasn't really after me."

"I don't think he was, at least not originally. I still think taking shots at you was just a ruse."

"So why have things changed?"

"I think your personal investigation must be getting close to the truth. You've got the killer rattled, so he decided to come after you, although that was a pretty amateurish way to do it."

"I could have gone off the road and been killed."

"But it was hardly foolproof as events showed. I think it was more in the nature of a warning than an actual attempt on your life." Thorndike frowned. "But I think you should leave this case to the police from now on. We don't want to have a third death."

"I don't either, especially mine. But if I'm getting so close . . ."

" . . . you think you might catch the killer before he gets you."

"That was my thinking."

She shook her head. "Too dangerous, Charles."

"I have an old friend of mine at Yale seeing if any faculty members know more about what happened there ten years ago. He's going to give me a call when he finds out something. There can't be anything dangerous about me answering the phone, can there?"

Thorndike sighed. "No, I suppose not. But don't go acting on any information you receive. Come straight to me. We'll handle it."

"Fine." Charles winced as he moved his leg off the footstool.

"Are you sure you don't want to go to the emergency room?"

"No need. I'm a fast healer."

"Every man I've ever worked with has believed that. His arm could be hanging by a thread, and he'll say, 'No problem, it'll heal by morning.'"

Charles decided to change the subject. "Did the people in experimental psychology have any idea who stole their precious rat?"

"Not a clue. During the school year, the lab is full of students and faculty, but in the summer, they just have a couple of students to feed and clean up after the animals. No one is there most of the day, and the door is generally left unlocked. Anyone at the school could have figured out how to make off with Freud."

"Did anyone see someone who didn't belong hanging around the area?"

Thorndike shook her head. "But it's pretty empty over there, and it could have been done at night."

"Well, thanks for bringing me the information," he said, starting to stand up.

She waved him back down. "Stay there. Rest your leg. In fact staying in the house resting your leg might be all you should do for the next couple of days."

Charles nodded, looking somber. Thorndike reached over and gave his shoulder a squeeze.

"Don't worry. We'll get this solved before too long."

Charles studied her face to see if she really believed that, but all he could see there was sympathy for him.

Chapter Twenty-Eight

The next morning a loud knocking on his front door awakened Charles. He rolled out of bed and groaned as he put weight on his injured leg. He hobbled down the hallway and pulled open the front door. Greg Wasserman stood there in his running gear bouncing up and down.

"Did you oversleep?" he asked, his voice vaguely accusatory.

"I hurt my leg. I won't be able to run today."

"Okay," he said, turning to go away.

"Could you come in for a minute?" Charles knew he was about to do something Thorndike would not approve of, but how much danger could be in within the confines of his own home.

"I don't have much time. I have an early summer school class this morning."

"It won't take long. It's about Garrison Underwood."

Wasserman stood still, then walked into the hallway.

"The police have already asked me about the Opal College Chair. Did you tell them I was angry about losing it?"

"It's a murder investigation, Greg, I can't keep quiet about things."

Greg frowned like he only half accepted that. "So what did you want to talk about?"

"I found out yesterday that you had an argument with Yuri about the Opal Chair on the day Underwood died."

"That's right. What about it?"

"And Yuri told you that Underwood had already taken over my office." Charles waited to see if Greg would agree to having that knowledge, but he remained impassive. "And I'm betting that you went right from Yuri's down to my office to talk with Underwood."

Greg stood there looking into the distance as thought Charles were telling him an irrelevant and not very entertaining story.

"I think you tried to convince Underwood to give up the chair, and he refused. In fact, he probably did more than that, he laughed at you for thinking he would give up anything. Did he then turn away from you in contempt, and in a moment of rage, did you hit him over the head with the trophy?"

Greg's nostrils dilated and his hands clenched into fists. Charles wondered for a moment if his feeling of safety in his own home had been overly optimistic. Suddenly Greg let out a bitter laugh.

"You've got most of it right, Charles. I did go to see Underwood, and he refused to even consider my arguments for giving up the Opal Chair. He said that was part of his contract for coming here, and he wasn't about to surrender it. I tried to tell him how giving it to him was unfair, and he told me that the internal politics of a minor college were none of his affair."

Wasserman paused and took a deep breath.

"But I didn't hit him. I wanted to, God knows. I could even picture myself doing it, and see the look of surprise on his face when my fist smashed into it. But I didn't hit him, I just turned and walked away."

"You walked out of the office and down the stairs to the parking lot where you saw me."

He nodded. "And you immediately told me all about your problems with Underwood. I saw you as a fellow sufferer, that's why I suggested we run together."

"Did you see anyone hanging around in the hallway near my office when you arrived or when you left?"

"No. There was no one around."

"So someone killed Underwood in the time between when you left, and when I went back to my office. That's only a window of around fifteen minutes."

"I suppose." Greg checked his watch. "Look I have to get going if I'm going to squeeze in my run."

"You have to go to the police with this. I haven't told them anything about your meeting with Yuri. It would be better coming directly from you."

Greg paused and nodded. "I guess you're right. I'll go to the station right after class."

After Wasserman left, Charles went in the kitchen and put on the coffee. He slowly made his way down driveway to the mailbox and retrieved his *New York Times*. It was Saturday so he had no responsibilities at the soup kitchen, and the college wouldn't be open except for the rare summer class. He really had nowhere to go and nothing to do. As he put together his breakfast, he considered spending the day reading the new novel he'd purchase online by an author the critics kept promising would soon produce the great American novel of the first half of the twenty-first century. Although he had a bias toward nineteenth century literature and thought there had been a gradual decline since then, unlike many of his fellow specialists, he hadn't stopped reading at the year nineteen eleven, and he thought there had been several reputable novelist in the twentieth century.

He was just starting to savor the thought of a day reading at home, when the phone rang.

"Mr. Bentley?" an efficient female voice asked.

"That's right," he replied with a sinking feeling. The voice was always the same. He knew well what the message would be.

"Your father has been very restless for the last couple of days. He keeps asking for you."

So why don't you sedate him, Charles thought harshly, and immediately pushed the remark away.

"We were wondering if it would be possible for you to visit him some time today?"

"I can come down later this morning."

"Good," the voice said, obviously relieved. "We'll have him up in a chair, all ready to visit."

"Fine."

The nursing home his father was in was down in Pittsfield, about forty minutes away. It was an act of discipline, more a penance really, that got him to make monthly visits. It had nothing to do with affection, but with a sense of the responsibility he believed a son should have for his father. Since having several strokes in his late seventies, his father's mind had been muddled, and it was difficult to know what he understood about his situation or the role of those around him. But he had occasional instances of clarity, which Charles found even harder to handle.

Charles had promised his mother, virtually on her deathbed, that he would continue to look after his father. Fortunately, there was enough of the family money left in the estate to take care of expenses, and Charles hoped that his monthly visits were frequent enough to keep the staff on their toes. His younger brother, who lived in Palm Springs, had been retired for several years. Like his father, he had done well in finance, and also like his father, he cared little for other people. He always told Charles that he'd like to make the trip back east to see their Dad, but his bad back prevented his making such a prolonged flight. Charles would have found that excuse more convincing if several family members, who had visited his brother, hadn't commented on how active he stayed, playing eighteen holes of golf three times a week.

Finishing his breakfast, he slowly dressed. He found that putting on his pants required sitting on the bed and going through contortions to manipulate the garment over his stiff leg. Popping a couple of aspirin to ease the pain, he went out to his car and headed south, thankful that it wasn't his driving leg that was injured. He breathed deeply along the way, trying to relax his mind, although he knew that within a few minutes of seeing his father any Zen-like calm would rapidly disappear. Once again he thought, as he always did on making this trip, how parents are so skilled at pushing exactly the right buttons to turn their children, no matter what their age, into querulous, sulky adolescents.

He carefully parked his car between the white strips as if to prove that he was a visitor and not a patient. During his visits in recent years, he had become more and more aware that some of the patients, or residents, as the home preferred them to be called, were close to his age. This always made him resolve to stay fit and as healthy as possible because his definition of hell was to be residing in the same care facility as his father. As an act of kindness the staff would probably have them share a room, which would shorten both their lives.

Charles walked in the front door and went up to the receptionist's window, trying to ignore the faint smell of human frailty that permeated the perfumed air. A few minutes after announcing himself, an aide wearing a cheerful green uniform took him to his father's room.

Although he had seen his father many times since the strokes, he never ceased to be shocked by the wizened, emaciated old man who confronted him. Even though he was in his early eighties, he gave the appearance of being so old as to be timeless with his large brown eyes protruding above his sunken cheeks. He had always been so aggressively robust that it was difficult to recognize him in this faint sketch of the man.

"Horace! Horace!" his father exclaimed as he raised his head and saw him.

"I guess he doesn't recognize you," the aide said.

Charles smiled slightly. "Everyone is Horace to him."

His father recognized him well enough, all his life he had refused to accept Charles' decision to use his middle name. Even when everyone in the family, including his mother, called him Charles, his father insisted on addressing him as Horace. He only varied this by occasionally calling him Junior, especially when he had done something his father considered worthy of reprimand. It was his way of reminding him that his mistakes reflected badly on his father.

"It's Charles," he corrected after the aide left the room.

"Horace!" the feathery voice insisted.

"How are you doing, Dad?" he asked. He couldn't remember calling his father "Dad" more than a handful of times when he was well. Now that his father had no choice, Charles considered it an intimacy that served to reflect the chasm between them.

Hi father twisted his mouth inward as if he'd detected a bad smell. That was his usual reaction to questions about his condition or state of mind. Charles noted that his father's false teeth hadn't been put in, and a day-old stubble of beard darkened his face. He would mention both at the nurses' station on the way out, but doubted little would change. He'd have to visit every day to bring about a real modification of institutional behavior.

"Where is Ed?" his father asked.

"In Palm Springs," Charles replied.

His father sat for a moment pondering the answer until Charles wondered whether it meant anything to him.

"He should be here," his father said petulantly.

I can't disagree with that, Charles thought.

"We can't always have everything we want," Charles said.

His father gave him a look of disgust, which was probably exactly what that bromide deserved. Charles thought back to when his father had refused to help him financially to go to graduate school. Not because the money wasn't easily available, but because he considered it to be reading to no purpose. Scholarship to him was a pointless activity, barely better than a hobby. His father had happily paid for Ed to attend business school. With the help of his VA benefit and working part-time, Charles had made his way through, and he had never stopped being thankful that his father had forced him to become independent. He knew that only this separation had kept him from becoming a pale clone of his father like his brother Ed. Sometimes unintended consequences could be good ones.

His father reached out a wrinkled, claw-like hand and seized his arm. Charles fought the impulse to pull away.

"Remember," his father said, pausing as if for effect, "friends and family will always betray you."

"Don't you think it depends on how you've treated them?"

His father shook his head as if Charles words were just so many buzzing insects.

"They will *always* betray you."

Having made what he considered to be his definitive statement on the matter, his father seemed to recede back into the chair like a balloon deflating. Charles knew he would say nothing more for the rest of the visit. Indeed, he might be mostly silent for the next few days. The desire to express himself seemed to come in waves, which, once released, would leave him too exhausted to think or speak.

Charles sat with him for a half hour longer, then he quietly got up and left.

Chapter Twenty-Nine

By the time Monday morning rolled around, Charles was feeling somewhat better. He had spent most of Sunday reading the newspaper and his new novel, and although his injured leg had turned a variety of vibrant colors on the side that had hit the road, it was feeling much better. It still stiffened up when he sat for long periods of time, but quickly loosened into approximate normalcy when he began to walk. This was good, he thought, because it meant no trip to the hospital, and it also kept him from having to explain his fear of rats to all the women at the soup kitchen. Charles wasn't afraid to show weakness, but he liked his public weaknesses to be less embarrassing than terror at the sight of small furry animals.

He decided to leave early for the soup kitchen and stop off at the police station. He had given Greg Wasserman two full days to make his confession to the police about seeing Underwood shortly before his death, so it was time for his to find out if Lieutenant Thorndike had been informed. He drove into the center of town and parked by the old brick building that housed the police department and the courthouse. Inside he told the officer that he wanted to speak with Lieutenant Thorndike. The officer took his name and disappeared down a hallway. He was back in a minute and held open the door that separated the offices from the public areas.

The Lieutenant stood up when he entered her office and smiled.

"How nice of you to visit me here, Charles, usually I'm the one taking advantage of your hospitality. I'd offer you coffee, but I'd be embarrassed by the comparison to yours. I can get you a glass of pretty good water."

"No, thanks," Charles said taking the offered chair. "I just wanted to find out if Greg Wasserman came by to tell you about seeing Underwood."

The Lieutenant waved a sheet of paper. "He came in on Saturday afternoon when I was off duty. One of my sergeants took his statement. I've just finished reading it."

"Good. I told him he had to see you."

Thorndike looked puzzled. "How do you figure into this? Wasserman didn't mention you."

"The English Department secretary told me about it."

"Why didn't she mention it to us sooner?"

"She was on vacation when the murder happened, and Sheila, the student assistant, only happened to mention it to her several days after. You can't really blame Sheila, she's something of a special case."

The Lieutenant shook her head. "No matter how many times we say it, people just don't understand that in a murder investigation everything is important." She glanced down at Greg's statement on her desk. "Do you think he killed Underwood?"

"He's a hard guy to read. He keeps his emotions close to his chest, but I kind of doubt it. Remember, I saw him in the parking lot right after he left Underwood. I know it's hard to tell, but he didn't look like he had just murdered someone."

"His eyes weren't rolling wildly and he wasn't foaming at the mouth?" she asked with a grin.

Charles smiled slightly. "Like I said, it's hard to tell. But he didn't seem in any hurry to leave, and we had quite a long, coherent conversation. I think he would at least have seemed somewhat distracted after bashing someone's head in."

"What about this guy Yuri, the department chairman. He was in the building at the same time. Would he have had any motive to kill Underwood?"

"He was a bit annoyed by Underwood's low opinion of modern English novels, but otherwise I don't think so. He might not have been happy about Dean Carruthers forcing Underwood on the department, but he wouldn't be upset enough to commit murder."

"Have you heard anything from your friend at Yale, the guy who's checking into Underwood's history there?"

"Nothing so far."

"I interviewed Gould and Rhyser after I talked to you on Friday. Gould acted a bit nervous like you said, but if every person who acted nervous was guilty of something, we'd have more criminals than crimes. I'm inclined to believe them. They knew about Underwood's behavior, but weren't victims themselves."

"You're probably right. I'll get in touch with my contact at Yale in a couple of more days if I don't hear anything sooner."

"Where are you off to now?"

"It's my day at the soup kitchen."

Thorndike picked up the knife she used as a letter opener and balanced it in her hand.

"Keep your eyes open, Charles, there's someone out there looking to harm you. They may be doing it in a round about way, using a rat. But it could escalate. I suppose you wouldn't consider cancelling the gig at the soup kitchen?"

Charles thought of his promise to Karen that he would keep showing up.

"I think I'll be as safe there as I would be at home. Anybody could knock on my front door and shoot me when I answered. At least at the soup kitchen I'm around other people."

Thorndike nodded. "I figured you'd say that. You know, for a guy who looks like the poster boy for the fussy academic, you seem remarkably willing to take risks."

"I don't like being pushed around."

"Okay, but stay aware of your surroundings, and give me a call day or night if you see anything suspicious. Let me give you another copy of my card. My cell number is on it, and I'll answer it whenever it rings. It never goes to voicemail."

She reached across the desk with her card. Their fingers touched. Charles wasn't sure whether he'd imagined it, but it seemed as though hers lingered a bit longer than necessary.

Once at the soup kitchen, Charles helped John sets up the tables. Although still not garrulous, the man had moved on from his laconic demeanor of last week, and they exchanged a few standard pleasantries. Charles thought John had come to the conclusion that Charles was there to stay, so he may as well reach some accommodation with him. As he finished with the last table and began walking across the basement to where the serving tables were set up, he saw Karen standing there staring at his legs.

"You have a limp," she said. "I don't think you had that before."

"I overdid it with the yard work this weekend," Charles lied. He didn't like to lie, but there was no way he was going to confess the truth.

"Yes, you have to be careful about that at our age," she said carefully, as if not quite believing him.

They didn't say anymore until they were working next to each other on the serving line. During a lull, she turned to him and asked, "How are things going with the investigation into those murders up at the College?"

"Don't know. I haven't heard much about it. I guess I won't now that I'm retired."

"I suppose not. I think it's a real shame that the students won't get to benefit from that fine professor from England."

Something snapped! Perhaps it was his basic honesty asserting itself or maybe he was simply tired of hearing Underwood extolled. The words simply flowed out of him unfiltered.

"I don't think it's much of a loss. The man had a history of acting inappropriately with female students."

Karen's spoon paused briefly midway on its journey to the pan of peas, and a few seconds later, when the line had moved on, she turned back to Charles.

"My daughter the dentist had a problem with a professor like that in dental school," she whispered.

"I'm sorry to hear that. There's no justification for that kind of behavior."

"She was so upset she wanted to leave school in the middle of the semester. I convinced her to stay and bring charges against the professor. She won her case, and he ended up getting into a lot of trouble."

"Good for her."

Karen nodded. "She transferred to another school at the end of the year anyway. She wanted to get away from the publicity. But everything was fine for her after that."

Charles was doling mashed potatoes onto the next plate in line when the significance of what Karen had just said came home to him. The woman who had been Underwood's sex slave might never have go on to get her PHD or any other degree from Yale. After all the ruckus about Underwood, she might we have wanted to transfer to a school where she was less well known. So she could be on the faculty at Opal, because the suspects were no longer restricted to Rhyser and Gould. All female professors under forty had entered the pool.

He was so excited that it took a moment before he realized that Karen was talking to him.

"What was that?" he asked.

Karen took a shaky breath and started over.

"I know the last time we talked I suggested that we take some time to become friends before going out."

"That's right," he said with a sinking feeling in his stomach.

"Well, the thing is Rachel asked me if I'd like to double date tonight with her and her boyfriend. That's Rachel over there in the kitchen," Karen said, pointing with her spoon.

Charles followed the spoon and saw a slender woman in the kitchen struggling mightily to clean a large pot.

"It wouldn't be anything complicated. Just going to a movie and then out to dessert. The thing is I don't have a boyfriend, but I didn't really want to tell Rachel that. So I was wondering if you would come along just to sort of help me out." Karen bit her lower lip. "I sort of told her already that you were coming."

Charles looked into her pleading blue eyes. Clubbing a baby seal would have been easier than refusing her, so Charles agreed. How bad can it be, he told himself, after all we'll be with another couple. It was only when he was breaking down the last table with John a half hour later that he realized how unlikely it was that Rachel would not have know Karen didn't have a boyfriend. That was almost the first thing women come to know about each other.

Shoving the last table against the wall, he stood stock-still and gazed across the cellar at Karen who was carrying dishes into the kitchen like a proper, God-fearing housewife. A deadening feeling made his limbs grow limp, and his will to live seemed to leave his body. He had been scammed. He knew that he had been brought down by one of the lions of the Serengeti. For a moment he was tempted to walk across the room and tell her he had changed his mind. But he knew the look of disappointment in her eyes would be too much for him to bear. No, he'd lost this round, but he'd be sure not to have it happen again.

Chapter Thirty

After leaving the soup kitchen, he made his way to his office at the College. He sat at his desk feeling despondent about his upcoming date. He was angry with himself for being deceived by a pleading expression and an implausible lie. Two could play this game, he thought defiantly. Immediately, however, he realized that he disliked lying and his pleading expressions never rose above the pathetic. The only way he could survive this game was by running fast and far.

He was slumped in self-loathing when Nora Chapman appeared in the doorway. He waved her into his office. She would at least prove to be a diversion. She gingerly made her way to the chair in front of his desk, hands on her back to balance the large bulge in front.

"How goes the effort to secure your child's inheritance?" he asked.

"God. Don't ask. Garrison's family has come out of the woodwork now that he's gone."

"I thought he didn't have any."

"They're second cousins, can you believe it. Every one in England must be a second cousin to everyone else. How can that count?"

"It certainly seems to me that his child would take precedence."

"Yeah, but we've got to prove that first, don't we?"

"You mean you need to prove that Garrison is the father?"

"Right. We got to get some of his DNA before they put him in the ground, then have the baby tested as soon as she's born. We won't know anything for sure until then."

"Is there some doubt even in your mind?"

"Of course not, I was so faithful to Garrison that it hardly matters."

Not sure how to interpret that Charles stayed silent.

"Anyway, I've got another problem that I need your help with. I'm hoping that if you tell the police they won't be so angry with me for withholding information."

"What information have you withheld?"

"One night shortly before he left to come here, Garrison happened to mention that he knew a woman at Opal College by the name of Marie. Since I didn't know at the time that he planned to come to America and try to give me the slip, it didn't mean much to me."

"But it must meant something to you have after he was murdered."

"Sure. However, the police were making sounds like I might have had an accomplice who had killed Garrison for me. And who would be better for that role than one of his former jilted girlfriends? I figured this Marie and I would be arrested as a package if I admitted to knowing about her. She killed Garrison and I knocked off Sylvia. Then we could divide up the estate together."

Charles had to admit that it sounded like a pretty good plan. Thorndike might be inclined to see it that way.

"So what do you want me to do with this information?" he asked.

"Share it with the Lieutenant. But tell her that I have no idea who this Marie person is, and I had nothing to do with either murder. She likes you, and might listen if it comes from you."

"You might look more innocent if you told her yourself."

She shook her head. "Just the sight of me would have her reaching for her cuffs. No, do this for me, and I'll be eternally grateful."

Once more he got a pleasing expression, this time from a pregnant woman. How could he refuse?

"You have no idea who this woman might be?"

"Only that he got to know her the last time he taught in this country."

"The Lieutenant will still want to talk to you about this."

Nora pulled a card out of a pocket in her blouse. "She can reach me through my lawyer," she said, suddenly looking less needy.

When Nora Chapman had left the office, Charles looked down his list of faculty and staff. He's always liked the name Marie because that had been his wife's middle name. The only woman named Marie at the college was a Marie Faltz who worked in the financial aid office. Institutions of higher learning were not listed for members of the staff, so he had no idea of her education. He doubted she would be the person, but how could he be sure. He'd have to talk to her, but trying to do that conjured up all sort of embarrassing scenarios. Never fully comfortable talking with staff members in the first place since they tended to look down on faculty as being almost as clueless as students, he couldn't think of a good excuse to pay a visit to this woman he didn't know. Finally he decided that hewing as close to the truth as possible was the way to go.

Charles left his office and walked up the left side of the College quadrangle. It was a beautiful summer day, the sun was shining brightly but there was a comfortable breeze wafting over the hills. Small clusters of students either taking summer classes or doing work-study were scattered around the campus, bright bursts of color against the green. When he entered the administration building the dark shadows blinded him for a moment, and he struggled to read the directory that pointed the way to the financial aid office. He realized that he hadn't been there since the days when Amy was a student there.

At the bottom of the stairs he entered a large office filled with desks at which staff, mostly women, were diligently pouring over papers or studying computer screens.

"Can I help you?" the woman at the desk nearest the wall asked sharply as if to warn him that this was a place of business not window shopping.

"I wanted to see Marie Faltz?"

"Do you have an appointment?"

"No. But I'm a faculty member, and I just wanted to ask her a question."

"You're faculty?" the woman asked, as if he had just admitted to being on a sexual predators list.

"Yes, in the English Department. It's a quick question and won't take up much of her time."

The woman stood up and slowly made her way across the room. She bent over the woman who must have been Marie Faltz and said something. Marie glanced over at Charles and shook her head. He shifted nervously from foot to foot as if worried that he'd failed some kind of test. They conferred a few seconds more, after which Marie gave a resigned shrug. The other woman motioned for Charles to come over.

"What did you want to see me about?" the woman asked when Charles reached the desk. The other woman showed no intention of leaving. Perhaps, Charles thought, she expected him to make an improper suggestion and felt she might be needed as a witness. Now that he was close enough Charles could tell that this Marie was at least fifty, probably too old to be the woman in question. But he had no choice but to forge ahead.

"A friend of mine who teaches at Yale recently mentioned to me that he knew a woman named Marie who had been a student of his ten years ago and worked here. He didn't tell me the woman's last name, but I wondered if you could be that person."

The woman stared at Charles as if he was making no sense at all, then she gave a sharp laugh.

"I've been working here ever since I got out of high school over thirty years ago."

The other woman also began to chortle, and Charles knew that this would be a popular source of amusement around the communal lunch table.

"Sorry to bother you. I guess I have the wrong person." Feeling himself blushing, Charles turned on his heel and headed for the door. The only consolation he could take away from this embarrassment was that he hadn't mentioned his name.

As he approached the doorway, Wayne Ryder, the head of financial aid walked in.

"Why as I live and breath if it isn't Charles Bentley. To what do we own this honor?" he asked loudly, clapping a meaty hand on Charles shoulder.

Waves of white hair and a florid complexion made Wayne appear simultaneously dignified and dissipated. Charles considered him a hail-fellow-unfortunately-met.

"Nice to see you, Wayne," Charles said softly and tried to maneuver his way around the man's ample girth.

"Found any more bodies lately," he bellowed, and looked past Charles to see the reaction of the room to his attempt at humor. Charles heard a few sycophantic twitters.

"Not today," Charles said, making for the door.

Wayne said something that Charles couldn't catch but it caused a roar of laughter in the room. Charles scurried down the hall, away from the echoing sounds.

Once back in his office and feeling relatively safe, Charles took a deep breath and called Lieutenant Thorndike. When he got through,

145

he reported that Nora Chapman had told him. The Lieutenant definitely wanted to speak to Nora for herself so Charles relayed her lawyer's information.

"Nora thought that you might suspect that she and this Marie were accomplices. Tow angry girlfriends out for revenge."

"The thought crossed my mind," Thorndike said.

"The problem is that there is only one Marie working at Opal, and she has never been near Yale. I asked her."

"Maybe I should question her."

"Trust me. That is absolutely not necessary. She's a local woman who's worked at the college for thirty years," Charles said, not wanting the Lieutenant to get a whiff of his embarrassing episode.

"Okay," Thorndike said, puzzlement in her voice at Charles' insistence. "But I'm coming under some pressure from the Chief to arrest Wasserman. After all, he had means, motive, and opportunity. The only thing saving him is that he was teaching at the time Sylvia was killed. If I could find some way to link him and Nora together it would be ideal."

"That would be a peculiar couple. I think we're making this more complicated than it has to be."

"Yeah, I guess so, but right about now the complicated is starting to look simple. Say would you like to go out to dinner with me tonight and discuss the case?"

Charles paused, struggling to find some answer other than the truth.

"Sorry, I have a date tonight."

"A date," Thorndike said, as if she would never have associated the word with Charles.

"Yes. With one of the women who works in the soup kitchen."

"Huh. Well good for you. We'll make it some other time."

"Definitely. I'd like that."

Charles hung up the phone feeling lower than he had since his forced retirement. He had to go on a date with someone who had tricked him into it, rather than with a woman whom he actually had some interest in getting to know. He had made a fool of himself in front of a room of women of around his own age. And he felt for the first time that he might actually never come to find out who had killed Garrison Underwood and Sylvia.

Feeling an utter failure on so many fronts, he locked his office and went home.

Chapter Thirty-One

Charles pulled up in front of the neat cape cod. Although rather small, it appeared well kept, and the two garden beds on either side of the front porch were filled with early summer annuals, which he knew were high maintenance because they had to be replaced every year. Charles preferred perennials that with a little maintenance came back under their own stream providing satisfying results, while requiring little care or attention. He wasn't surprised that Karen would put in annuals. She struck his as the kind of person who would enjoy the process of gardening and rise to the yearly challenge.

Karen appeared at the front door wearing a colorful purple blouse with light tan slacks. She looked so stylish that Charles felt self self-conscious in his baggy chinos and threadbare shirt. Since Barbara's death, he hadn't bought much in the way of new clothes, only shopping at all when Amy visited and insisted on dragging him along to the mall. To offset his embarrassment, he thrust out his right hand holding a small bouquet of flowers. It had been so long since he dated that he didn't know if a man gave a woman flowers on a first date, but Karen had seemed traditional enough that he didn't think he could go wrong. Charles wondered what his male students presented to girls on first dates, probably nothing or perhaps a lid of marijuana. He wasn't sure how much a lid was, but it sounded intriguing.

"Oh, how beautiful," Karen exclaimed over the flowers, while Charles found himself smiling with inordinate pride. "Let me just get them into some water, and then we can go."

Charles followed her down the hall into the kitchen. Compared to his own kitchen, it was very modern, with granite countertops and stainless steel appliances.

"Your kitchen is very contemporary," Charles said, not sure whether that was meant to be a compliment or not.

"Thank you. It was my first big project after Stan died. I'd wanted to do the kitchen for a long time—it was sort of stuck in the seventies—but Stan always said that he as happy with the way it was. After he passed, I decided there was nothing stopping me from having it the way I wanted."

Charles nodded. He wondered how many changes Barbara would have made if he had been the first to go. Unlike his approach of settling for everything as it was, he had a feeling she would have modified the house and her way of life significantly. Would she already have remarried? He could easily imagine her doing so now that he thought about it. On the other hand, she might not want to be tied down again to someone with competing interest and goals. She'd have been free for the first time in over thirty years to be herself. The idea that he might have been a drag on Barbara's sponteneity momentarily depressed him.

"See. Don't they look nice?" Karen asked, holding up the flowers in a cut glass vase. "I'll put them right on the dining room table." She darted out of the room and returned a second later. "I guess we'd better go. We're supposed to meet Rachel and Jim at seven-fifteen."

The drive to the theatre only took ten minutes, and one compliment about her flower garden spurred Karen into talking about her gardening for the whole journey. Charles was pleased to note that he had been right, she was someone who gardened because she enjoyed the activity and was not just motivated by the colorful end result.

They found a place in the parking lot next to the small movie theatre, which was in the center of the downtown of Opalsville. One of the few private movie houses to survive, it got by because of the patronage of Opal College students and faculty who made it almost a point of pride to walk on its sticky floors and sit in the lumpy seats.

On the street inn front of the theatre stood Rachel, whom Charles had last seen scouring a pot almost as large as she was. Next to her was a large man, at least six two, who had a girth to match his height. His personality had apparently developed to meet his size as well because when he was introduced to Charles as Jim, he clapped a meaty hand on Charles' shoulder and said he was pleased to meet a college professor.

"A retired professor," Charles pointed out.

"I'm sure they never take the professor out of the man. It's like me—I'm in construction, and I still work—but even if I got out of the business, a contractor is what I would always be. It's the way I see the world. They can never take the contractor out of the man."

"I'm sure that's true," Charles said cautiously.

"But that doesn't mean I'm not happy to mix with all kinds," he said, beaming at Charles, as if he were a mongrel being allowed to fraternize with the show winners.

"So am I," Charles agreed.

Jim looked a bit uncertain at that but then smiled as he studied the marque.

"Seems like the girls have got us going to a romantic comedy. Not exactly my cup of tea, but maybe it's more yours," he said, looking askance at Charles.

"No, I prefer serial killer movies. I like the challenge of trying to discover our common humanity."

Jim appeared puzzled, then brightened. "Yeah, I like those action flicks myself."

Charles and Jim purchase the tickets, and they went into the lobby. Jim made a beeline to the refreshment counter and purchased the largest bucket of popcorn, asking for extra butter, and got himself the largest cup of soda. Rachel shook her head at the offer of soda, and Jim looked hurt.

"Rachel worries about Jim's health," Karen whispered.

"I would, too."

"He's already had one coronary event."

"I can imagine."

"But whenever she says anything, he just brushes her off and says that you only live once."

"Trite but true," Charles said. "Still it doesn't prove his point."

Karen gave him a puzzled glance.

"I mean even if you only go around once, you might prefer to go around able to do the things you want to do rather than as a barely ambulatory invalid," he explained.

"I try to stay fit. I go to the gym four days a week."

"I run," Charles said, feeling a flush of guilt at exaggerating his accomplishments.

"Doesn't that bother your knees?"

"Not yet," he replied, making a note to check with Greg on whether that as a future complication

Charles discovered that fortunately he was not seated next to Jim. He had Rachel on one side and Karen on the other. Jim offered his popcorn once, but when Karen and Charles refused, he horded it, only sharing it occasionally with Rachel. When the film was over, Charles had to admit that he'd enjoyed himself. Although the characters were a bit hackneyed, going back at least to the Commedia dell'arte, the plot was spritely and the story well acted. Rachel and Karen spent a couple of minute exclaiming over the movie, while Jim rolled his eyes and winked at Charles. Charles ignored the winks and added his own positive remarks, which earned him a disapproving glance from the other male in the group.

They stood on the sidewalk in front of the theatre. The two women were debating the merits of various places to go for dessert. Charles stood there entranced by the amount of mental energy woman could expend on such a mundane question, while Jim paced back and forth impatiently as if he had several more appointments yet to come this evening.

"Let's go, ladies, while the night is still young," he finally said, his exasperation showing through his attempt at humor.

Rachel gave him a reproving glance. "We're making progress. We've narrowed it down to The Mansion or Leonora's."

"Which do you think, Charles," Karen said, grabbing his hand and doing a little twirl to stand in front of him with a teasing smile on her face. "Where should we . . ."

Time compressed. Charles was aware of hearing a loud noise from somewhere in front of him. In the same instance, the smile disappeared from Karen's face and her eyes rolled up into her head. She lunged forward into Charles. He grabbed her as she slumped down like a puppet whose strings had been cut. He couldn't hold the dead weight, and he lowered her gently to the sidewalk. It was then he noticed the blood billowing from the front of her purple blouse. There was a roaring in his ears. In the distance someone screamed. Another voice shouted, "Dial 9-1-1!"

"Karen, I'm sorry," Charles whispered to the unconscious body. "It's all my fault."

Chapter Thirty-Two

Charles sat in the waiting room at the hospital. He waited and thought. He and Rachel and Jim had been interviewed by police officers at the scene, although none of the three could give a very comprehensive description of what had happened. From what Charles had overheard from the others the police questioned, those standing in front of the movie at the time of the shooting, no one had seen the shooter who apparently, according to the direction the police had been pointing, was at the end of an ally across from the movie.

After the police were done with them, Charles, Jim, and Rachel stood looking at each other for a moment as if unsure what to do next.

"I think we should go to the hospital to see how Karen is doing," Charles suggested. Rachel quickly nodded agreement.

"I'd like to, but I've got a late appointment tonight and have to get home," Jim said.

"Really?" Rachel said, giving him a hard stare.

Jim shrugged apologetically. "Business is business."

Rachel turned away from him. "Will you drive me to the hospital?" she asked Charles.

He agreed. He waved goodbye to Jim who was already walking toward the lot. Rachel didn't even glance in his direction. Charles had a feeling that their relationship had reached a sudden end. Not staying around out of concern for a friend was a major faux pas, even if there wasn't much in terms of practical help that Jim could have provided.

"What did you mean when you said 'It was all my fault?'" Rachel asked as they were driving toward the hospital.

"What are you talking about?"

"Right after you laid her on the ground, you apologized to her and said it was all your fault. What was your fault?"

Charles paused. He didn't remember saying that. It must have been something that came out automatically in the heat of the moment. Explaining this was going to be tricky.

"I've been sort of peripherally involved in the two murders that took place on campus, and that's led to someone making a couple of half-hearted attempts to kill me."

"Someone is trying to kill you?"

"The police aren't certain, but it is a possibility."

"Someone is trying to kill you, and you went out with us this evening. I can see why you took the blame, that bullet was meant for you."

"Probably," Charles admitted weakly.

"What do you mean *probably*? Do you think someone with a rifle was out there gunning for Karen?"

"No, I guess not."

"Yeah, *I guess not*," she said with obvious sarcasm. "You should feel guilty. If she dies, it will be on your head."

"I didn't pull the trigger. That's the person who's really responsible."

"Maybe you didn't pull the trigger, but you put her in the line of fire."

Charles sighed. "Yes. You're right."

When they got to the hospital, Rachel marched into the emergency room and wanted to know where they could find Karen Melrose. When the clerk at the emergency room desk wanted to know if she was family, Rachel said in a very convincing tone that she was her sister.

"You aren't her sister, are you?" Charles asked, once the woman had gone off to check on Karen.

"No, Charles." Rachel sounded exasperated. "But there's no way I'm letting some trivial hospital rules keep me from Karen."

The clerk returned a few minutes later to tell them Karen was in surgery. She gave them directions how to get there.

Rachel marched off, apparently not caring whether Charles came along or not. He had to hurry to keep up with her, but he was determined to find out Karen's condition. They went down a long hall and up a set of stairs that took them into another building. Finally, they saw a sign that said "surgery" and Rachel stopped at the desk.

"Can you tell what the condition is of Karen Melrose?" Rachel asked, her voice shook indicating she expected to hear the worst.

The nurse checked a computer screen. "She's still in surgery. Are you family?"

"I'm her sister," Rachel lied again.

"You can have a seat in the waiting room. We'll come and get you when we have some information."

Charles turned in the direction of the waiting room right across the hall.

"I'm going to sit out here," Rachel said, pointing to a chair in the hall. "You can go wherever you want. Why don't you go home, that might make things safer for all of us."

"You'll need a ride home."

"I can always call my daughter."

"I'll sit in the waiting room. I'd like to know how Karen is doing."

"Suit yourself." Rachel plopped down in the hall way chair.

Charles went into the waiting room. It was painted a soothing shade of lavender, and filled with simple but functional furniture. In the corner was a table with magazines. Charles went over to browse through them. Even in the worst of times, he knew reading could be comforting. But aside for a couple of medical publications, the magazines all dealt with either automobiles or hunting. Considering the reasons why people ended up in surgery, he thought there was a delicious irony in that. He sat down with one of the medical journals, but soon found his mind wandering.

Was he really responsible for Karen's injury? Had he shown a reckless disregard for the welfare of others by going out on a date when he might be the target of a killer? But even Lieutenant Thorndike hadn't warned him not to go on his date. No one had taken these threats on his life very seriously—up until now. He sat there stewing about his responsibility, but somewhere along the way he must have dozed off because he wasn't aware of another presence in the room until someone touched his arm.

"Charles," Lieutenant Thorndike said softly, giving his arm a gentle squeeze.

Charles bolted upright in the chair, afraid that once again his inattention had put someone at risk.

"Easy, easy," Thorndike said.

Charles shook his head as if shaking could get everything back into its proper place. Suddenly his eyes popped open wide, and he searched her face for any sign of bad news.

"Have you heard anything about Karen's condition?"

"She's going to be fine. The bullet hit her high in the back on her right side. There was a lot of bleeding, but she should recover completely. There wasn't even any serious damage to her shoulder."

Charles breathed a deep sign of relief and felt tears comes into his eyes.

"You really care about her?" asked the Lieutenant.

"I hardly know her, but I don't want her dying in my place. I shouldn't have taken her out on a date in the first place with someone gunning for me."

"Neither one of us took the previous threats on your life seriously enough. But this one was different. If Karen hadn't stepped in front of that bullet, given your relative positions and size differences, it probably would have hit you in the heart. This time the shooter was in earnest."

"Someone thinks I know more than I do."

"Or thinks you're on the brink of finding out."

"What should I do?"

"Getting out of town for a few days might be a good idea."

"How will that help? The killer will just wait around until I get back."

"He may decide that you've been scared off and leave you alone. Plus in that time our investigation might get somewhere. We're still canvasing the neighborhood where Sylvia was shot hoping to find someone who saw something. I'm also going to call Nora in for another interview, just in case she had an accomplice. And maybe by then your contact at Yale might have come up with the name of the person Underwood mistreated so badly during his time there."

Charles frowned. "I guess I could go visit my daughter for a few days."

"How long?"

"I doubt I could stand more than two. Between her husband and the boys, I'm exhausted after a couple of days. The boys run around like demented savages and Jack the Philistine wants to tell me in detail about wealthy management."

"Now that you're retired, wealth management might be more relevant to you."

"Not when it comes from Jack. He can never separate the forest from the trees enough to give you an overall sense of what he's talking about."

Thorndike grinned, and Charles thought that she really was a very attractive woman.

"I came here with Karen's friend Rachel. She was waiting out in the hall. She needs a ride home."

"I talked to her first, and had an officer take her home."

Charles nodded his thanks. "She was pretty angry with me. Wouldn't even stay in the same room. She thinks I was irresponsible endangering Karen and herself."

"Like I said, I'm more to blame than you are. I should have taken those threats more seriously." Lieutenant Thorndike stood up and looked down at Charles. "Are you ready to go home?"

He looked at his watch and saw that it was well past one o'clock.

"Yes, I guess it's time. When do you think Karen will be allowed to have visitors?"

"Probably not for a day or two. And I would recommend waiting a while until people's tempers have cooled. Maybe until after you come back from your daughter's.

"Good idea," Charles said, getting to his feet. "Right now I'm no one's favorite."

Thorndike patted him on the shoulder. Her touch was comforting.

"I'm sure some folks still like you."

Chapter Thirty-Three

Lieutenant Thorndike followed him home, and checked out the security in the house, locking all the windows and checking the doors. When she was done, she'd given him a reassuring smile and said that a cruiser would be coming past the house on an hourly basis to look out for intruders. She thought he was safe for now, and he should try to get a good night's sleep. Charles tried, however, the next morning he felt as if he hadn't rested at all. His body ached from spending the night tossing and turning. He'd awakened a couple of times from a shallow sleep in a cold panic, reliving the moment when Karen had slumped into his arms. Guilt and fear were proving a potent combination.

When Greg came to the door at seven, Charles debated what to tell him. Finally he decided that the truth might give him some valuable information as to whether the physicist had been involved in the shooting. Charles doubted that was the case, but you never knew. So he stood just inside the doorway for safety and told Greg about last night's shooting. He said he was going away for a couple of days and wouldn't be available to run.

Greg ran in place and began looking over his shoulder as if he might be in the line of fire if the murderer was trying for a second shot.

"Yeah, I guess going away is a good idea," he said with a trace of nervousness. "We should probably put off running together until they catch the killer."

Charles nodded. "That might be best," he said, amused that he had finally managed to rattle the always-composed physicist.

Well, he didn't have anything to do with it, Charles thought to himself as he closed the door. Greg might be a lot of things, but a good actor wasn't among them. He had been genuinely frightened.

Charles had breakfast after a quick dash to his mailbox for *The New York Times*, during every moment of which he'd expected to hear the crack of a gunshot and feel his body go numb. But some risks were outweighed by the result. And having the *Times* with his breakfast was one such important result. As he ate his cereal, had coffee, and read about the misery throughout the world, he began to feel somewhat more optimistic. Perhaps it as because the world situation was so much worse than his own, but it was also because Karen was going to recover, he was still alive, and the chances of catching the murderer were no worse than before all of this happened.

When he was sure that his grandsons would have been delivered to preschool or kindergarten, whichever they were in, he called his daughter.

"Hi Dad," she said, not attempting to conceal her surprise. "What's wrong?"

"Nothing. Does something have to be wrong for me to call my only child?"

The moment of silence on the other end made Charles realize how infrequent his calls to Amy actually were. Almost always, she was the one who initiated contact. Barbara had been the one who made the obligatory phone calls, allowing Charles to squeeze in a couple of shouted comments. After her death, he had not taken up the slack, leaving it to Amy, as if it were the woman's job to hold their tiny family together. He resolved that he would be better about this in the future.

"Well, it's good to hear from you anyway."

"I was thinking—if it's okay with you, that is—I'd like to come to visit for a couple of days."

"Are you *sure* nothing's wrong?"

"Of course there isn't. Well, maybe I have been feeling a bit at loose ends lately now that I'm retired. I just thought this would be a good opportunity to see the boys, and Jack, of course."

Again there was a moment of silence. "Has Karen Melrose still been pursuing you?"

"Do you think I'm running away from something," he said, trying to sound hurt.

"It's just that I usually have to call you and cajole you onto visiting. It's not like you to take the initiative."

"As a matter of fact, Karen and I did go out last night. I didn't think it was a big success. I'm not sure how she felt about it." Although he could certainly make an educated guess, Charles thought.

"So you don't want to be around for a few days in case she calls you back for an encore."

"That's something like the idea." And a remote possibility, Charles thought.

"Well, of course, you're welcome. The boys always like a chance to see their grandpa on my side. They see Jack's father often enough. You'll be a nice change of pace."

Charles recalled that Jack's father was a very successful corporate lawyer in Boston. He'd only met him at the time of the wedding, and his impression was of a florid, portly man who was confident and self-satisfied. Charles wondered how he managed to cope with the grandsons, who were certainly no respecters of privilege.

"How about I aim at getting there by lunch? I can take you out if you'd like?"

"Why don't we have a quiet lunch in? I have a lot of thing to do this morning, and I won't feel like getting fixed up to go out."

"That's fine."

"Safe travels then."

Charles hung up the phone. He gazed longingly out the sliding door at the patio where he would like to be sitting. He doubted the shooter would try the same trick twice, but he didn't dare risk it. Although he wasn't terrified, last night's experience had made him duly cautious. Life might not always hold a lot of charms for him, but he didn't want to shuffle off without knowing who had killed Garrison Underwood and tried to kill him.

He went upstairs to his bedroom and threw enough clothes for two days in his bag and packed his toiletries. He couldn't remember when he had done this last, and realized that it must have been over six months since he had last visited Amy and the grandchildren. Again, he made a silent resolution to do better about that.

He went through the house and made certain everything was locked. He didn't want to be surprised by an intruder when he returned home. He went out and put his bag in the car. Attempting to look casual, he glanced around the neighborhood, on the lookout for anyone spying on his home. The neighborhood appeared as innocent as always. Driving away, he turned down a series of quiet residential streets to make sure he wasn't being followed. He thought he must have been followed from his home last night for the shooter to have had time to stake out the movie theatre, and he wasn't going to put Amy and the children at risk by allowing that to happen again. When his circuitous route didn't reveal anyone following him, he eventually got back on a main secondary road and headed south toward the Massachusetts Turnpike.

Approximately three and a half hours later, he was knocking on Amy's front door. She opened the door and stood there in jeans and a sweater with her hair pulled back in a severe but functional ponytail. She looked so young that for one disconcerting moment, Charles saw her as the girl she had been, forgetting that she was in her thirties and a married mother of two.

"You made excellent time," she said, giving him a hug. "You can put your bag in Jack's study. You remember that doubles as a guest room."

Charles went up the stairs and into the room at the end of the hall. A large desk with an oversized computer dominated the room. In one corner was a small sleeper sofa that Charles remembered as having a bar that hit him right in a sensitive part of his back when he tried to sleep at night. Ah, well, he thought, I can survive anything for two nights, and it's better than being shot at.

When he came back downstairs, he heard Amy at work in the kitchen, and went to join her.

"I hope you don't mind tuna fish sandwiches for lunch."

"I'd be disappointed if we didn't have them. You ate them almost everyday through high school."

Amy laughed. "I'm lucky I didn't get mercury poisoning. I don't eat them nearly as much now, but one in a while I get a hankering for some comfort food." She placed the sandwiches on a plate and poured a glass of milk for herself. "Do you want some of this morning's left over coffee?"

"Sounds great," Charles said, settling into a chair around the kitchen table.

Amy and Jack had repurposed the dining room as a playroom for the boys and always ate in the kitchen. When Charles once asked Amy what they did when they had adults over for a dinner party she just rolled her eyes. "We don't do that much anymore. We mostly meet our adult friends at kids' events like birthdays and sports activities."

"Don't you miss normal adult conversation about ideas and events of the day?" he'd asked.

"I do. But I don't think Jack does. He only has two topics of conversation: the boys and financial investing."

"Doesn't Jack have any friends? What about the people he works with?"

"He says they're competitors, not friends."

They'd had this discussion six months ago, and it had been the only time Amy had expressed even a whiff of criticism of Jack. Charles had always been amazed that she seemed to think him perfect.

"This is great!" Amy said, chewing her sandwich with obvious delight. You really need comfort food once in a while."

Charles nodded, but thought that all this talk of comfort food required more examination.

"How are things going in your life?" he asked.

"Great! The boys are doing well in school, and both of them have gone out for peewee soccer. It's a great way for them to burn off their after school energy. Jack just got a promotion at work. He's the supervisor of his territory now."

"Does he have to spend more time at work?"

"Yes. But he's very good about taking weekends off to be with the boys, and he comes to all the other activities he possibly can."

"And what about you? Are you happy with your life?"

Amy shrugged. "My life is the boys. That's almost inevitable at this stage."

"I always forget. What grades are the boys in?"

"Jack Jr. is in second grade, and Kevin is in first."

"So they're both away for a good part of the day."

Amy gave him a piercing glance. "I know where this is going. You're wondering what I do with all my time when the boys are in school. Well, there's lots of housework to do, plans to be made, shopping, and I have to be ready to pick the boys up when school gets out to take them to their various activities. I don't have time to get a job."

"Would you like to have one?" Charles asked.

Amy paused as if stumped by the question, then she resumed in a flatter tone.

"Some days I think I would. Just a chance to get out of the house and be with adults in a productive environment would add a lot of spice to my life. Plus I worked hard for my degree, I'd like to have a chance to use it."

"Couldn't you look into a part time job? That way you could be home for the boys after school. You could even volunteer, become a docent in the museum, then you would have very limited hours."

"Or I could work in the soup kitchen," she said with a teasing smile.

Charles smiled back. "There are worse things."

Her face became sober. "Jack wouldn't be happy about that, he's kind of old fashioned. His mother was a full-time homemaker and still is. Jack feels that any husband worth the title should be able to support his wife and family. He gets that from his Dad."

"I'm sure," Charles said drily.

"It's not necessarily a bad thing."

"Supporting your family is admirable, but not letting your wife develop her talents isn't."

Amy shrugged, and they changed the topic. After lunch, Charles went upstairs and took a nap on the sofa in his room. When he awoke he was surprised to see that an hour had passed. Rousing himself, and feeling a little bit guilty at sleeping in the middle of the day, he went in the bathroom and washed his face. Then he retrieved the novel he had brought, and read until he heard Amy come home with the boys. Girding he loins he went downstairs into the dining room that had been converted into a playroom.

"Grandad!" Jack Jr. shouted, running towards him.

Charles squatted down, hearing his knees crack, and Jack gave him a big hug. Kevin, younger and always a bit shyer, came over more slowly and hugged him on the other side. Although the boys still liked the physical contact of wrestling around, during his last couple of visits Charles had noted that now the boys wanted to talk, to tell him lengthy and sometimes non- sequential stories of their day. This time was no different as they settled on the broken down sofa in the playroom, and each boy began to talk with urgency. They interrupted each other so frequently that Charles finally had to impose order so only one spoke at a time. If one went on too long, a few interspersed tickles would soon distract him and give the other boy a chance to speak.

Thinking back to When Amy had been that age, it seemed to him that, although she liked to talk, there had always been something a bit more disciplined about her, as if the art of conversation had come to her earlier. Although Charles was a great believer in female equality, his discussions with friends who had both boys and girls had convinced him that there were physiological differences between the sexes that could be mitigated but not eliminated by upbringing. Whether these differences made one gender superior to the other depended on the type of society they lived in. Modern society, having less use for upper body strength and physical aggressiveness and more for fine motor skills and the ability to negotiate, might be showing a bias in favor of women that didn't bode well for his grandsons.

He played with the boys until their mother took them into the kitchen for a snack. When they came back, they settled on the couch and watched a video that the boys had seen before but still apparently enjoyed. Despite their vocal guidance as to what was going to happen next, Charles had difficulty following the plotline. When six o'clock came around there was the sound of the garage door opening, and like little automatons that boys simultaneously shouted "Daddy's home!" and made a beeline to the door from the garage into the kitchen.

Charles debated joining the greeting line, but finally decided to stay where he was until Jack put in an appearance. A few minutes later Jack came into the playroom with the boys dancing around his feet like small attendants to the king. Jack gave Charles an embarrassed smile as if to suggest that he couldn't do anything about such adoration. Charles thought he reveled in it.

"Charles," Jack finally said, reaching out his hand over Kevin's head.

"Jack," Charles replied giving it a firm shake.

"Good of you to come."

"Good of you to have me."

"Why don't we go into the living room? That's the one place off-limits to the boys. Would you like a drink?"

"A scotch would be nice."

Jack nodded and headed back into the kitchen with the boys trailing along behind him. Charles went across the hall to the living room. It was furnished rather formally with a sofa and three chairs in a conversational grouping. Clearly it had been decorated at a time when Amy had expected to have more adult gatherings. Before she chose to devote her life completely to her husband and boys.

Jack came in and handed him a drink, then settled down in the chair across from him.

"We'll have to drink fast, dinner is almost ready. Things have to run like clockwork around here with the boys. They're very much creatures of habit, and seem to have little internal clocks that tell them when everything has to happen."

Charles nodded and sipped his drink. He wondered how long to wait until asking Jack about work and unleashing a monologue that would last through dinner.

"I hear there was some excitement out your way. Someone was killed in your office."

Charles admitted that was the case.

"Have the police got any leads?"

"They have a few suspicions, but so far I don't think they have a fully coherent view of what happened." Charles thought it best not to mention the second murder.

Jack shook his head. "Everywhere is dangerous today. There's not enough law and order."

Charles nodded, not wanting to provoke a discussion that would doubtlessly reveal differences of opinion between them.

"And now you've retired," Jack said, as if somehow that was a consequences of the murder. Although, Charles had to admit, it was in a way, Jack had no reason to think so.

"That's right. It was time to pull the trigger," he said, consciously using a phrase that he thought Jack would appreciate.

"What are you going to do with yourself? Of course, it isn't like college teaching is exactly a full time job."

Charles gave him an inquiring look.

"I mean you have summers off, and holidays, and you don't exactly put in a forty hour workweek. So retirement isn't as much of a shock as it would be for most men."

"I suppose that's true." Charles admitted, realizing his manhood had been called into question.

"I can't imagine retiring," Jack said, taking a long pull on his drink as if the very idea stressed him. "I need the challenge of competing in the workplace. One thing about financial management, the numbers don't lie, you always know whether you're being successful or not. I guess that isn't true in college teaching."

"Yes, it's hard to tell what kind of influence you're having on the students even in the short run. And in the long run, who knows what kind of an impact, if any, your course will have on their lives."

"That would frustrate the hell out of me. I need to know what I've achieved at the end of every day. I want it to be quantifiable. Otherwise I'd feel that I was just wasting my time."

Feeling that his career had just been written off as a waste of time, Charles decided to shift to a safer subject.

"It must be hard for you when the stock market is down like it's been lately."

"That just means there's a buying opportunity, Charles. You buy when the market is down and hang on as it goes up."

"I see. But your clients must get nervous seeing their nest eggs shrink."

Jack rattled the ice in his glass and gave a chuckle. "That's why so much of my job is hand holding. I have to support people through difficult times, sometimes even drag them kicking and screaming into acting in their own self interest."

"I guess people aren't as naturally rational as Adam Smith thought."

Jack nodded blankly, and Charles wondered if he'd ever heard of Adam Smith. Jack had gone to college, but perhaps business programs no longer emphasized the classics.

Amy popped her head into the living room. "Supper's on, boys. Get it before it gets cold."

Charles and Jack got to their feet and headed toward the kitchen.

"Amy mentioned to me that you've gotten a recent promotion. How is your new job different from the old?" Charles asked.

He knew he'd just established the conversation for dinner: safe but boring.

• • • •

CHARLES WOKE UP EARLY the next morning. He lay on his back thinking about what course of action to take when he returned home. He had called Nancy, the woman in charge of the soup kitchen, and told her he wouldn't be available for a few days. He had every intention of returning, although he wondered what his reception would be like once people knew of his role in Karen's shooting. The concern kept him from falling back to sleep, and when he heard a footfall in the hall around six o'clock, he decided to go downstairs to see if a cup of coffee was available.

When he went into the kitchen, Jack was sitting at the table, already dressed in a business suit, eating a bowl of cereal. He was reading *The Wall Street Journal,* which shattered Charles' hopes for *The New York Times.* Jack looked up and gave him a restrained smile.

"You're up early."

"I never sleep well in a new place."

Jack nodded. "There's coffee if you want some."

Charles poured himself a cup and sat down on the other side of the table. He didn't want to sit across from Jack with nothing to do, as though he expected to be engageed conversation. His hand was inching toward the back of the *Journal* when Jack put down his paper and stared at him.

"Amy told me that you thought she should get a job."

"I didn't say that. I merely suggested that if she wanted one, she should give it some thought. Did the two of you discuss it?"

"Discuss it? Of course not."

Of course not, you coward, Charles thought.

"She's too busy with the boys right now to think about a job. Since my promotion I'm getting paid enough to easily support us and set aside money for both boys to go to a good college."

"So Amy isn't interested in working right now?"

"No, she isn't,"Jack said with defiance.

Charles shrugged. "You know some day, not much more than a decade from now, your boys are going to go off to those fine colleges you'll be paying for, and Amy is going to be all by herself with you. And she's going to think about all these years when you told her she could do without a job, and she might well decide that now she can do without you."

Jack blushed a bright red and his hands clenched. Charles wondered if Jack was likely to last out another decade with such barely controlled anger. Finally the man smiled humorlessly.

"You know I used to always tell Amy that she should encourage you to come out more often. They get to see my parents a lot, and I wanted them to have a balanced view of the family. Whenever I said that, Amy would give me kind of a funny look, like I should be careful what I wished for. Now I understand what she meant."

"Perhaps she was right," Charles replied.

Jack stood up abruptly, dumped what was left of his cereal in the sink, and strode out of the room. A few seconds later Charles heard the garage door go up and the car engine start. Charles thought that some client was going to get less than his expected amount of hand holding today.

He poured himself a second cup of coffee and thought about how this had not been a good beginning to the day.

Chapter Thirty-Four

F ifteen minutes later Amy came down and said good morning to her father.

"The boys will be down in ten minutes, and it will be a zoo in here. You might want to have your breakfast now or wait until they go."

"I'll have a bowl of cereal now," Charles said.

Amy got him a bowl and a glass of orange juice. Charles poured out some of the same cereal Jack had been eating.

"Did you see Jack before he left?" she asked.

Charles nodded.

"Did you discuss anything important?" she asked giving him a meaningful glance.

"Let's talk about it after the boys go."

Charles had just finished his breakfast when he heard the thumping of feet on the stairs, he stood up in battle position as the boys tore into the room.

"Grandpa!" they both shouted, giving him hugs.

"Now I'm going in the front room for a while to read the paper," he said, immediately standing up and tucking the *Wall Street Journal* under his arm. "You eat and get ready for school." Giving each boy a pat on the head, he left the room.

Although he found less of interest in *The Wall Street Journal* than in the *Times*, Charles managed to occupy himself until the boys came into the room wearing their backpacks and gave him a kiss before Amy drove them to school.

"Will you be here again tonight, Grandpa?" Jack Jr. asked.

"We'll see," Charles replied.

Amy gave him a pointed look and followed the boys out to the car. Charles went into his room and carefully packed his things. He put his bag by the front door and resumed his seat in the living room. Five minutes later Amy returned. She eyed his bag as she sat down across from him.

"Planning to run away again?" she asked.

Charles shrugged. "It might be for the best. Jack really doesn't care for me."

"What did the two of you talk about?"

"Jack made it quite clear to me that being a wife and mother is more than enough for you, and that I should mind my own business."

"We did have a brief discussion of my getting a job last night," Amy admitted.

"Sounded to me more like he gave you orders." Charles paused, aware that he was getting close to saying too much, then doing it anyway. "I don't know what you see in him, Amy."

"I see a man who loves his family and isn't afraid to take responsibility for them."

Charles listened carefully to her tone of voice. "Do you mean unlike me? Do you really doubt that I loved you and your mother?"

"No. It's the second part that was always a problem for you—the taking responsibility. You liked having a family there and loved us, but you always avoided getting too involved."

"How can you say that? I did my share of childcare from the time you were an infant, and I was always there when you needed anything."

Amy smiled. "You were always there, Dad, for all the little things. And don't think I don't appreciate it. But whenever there were big decisions to be made, I always knew that it would be up to Mom. Where we lived, where I would go to school, whether we would travel on vacation: they were all decided by Mom."

Charles frowned, trying to remember exactly what things had been like.

"I always expressed an opinion."

"Yes. You were always good at leading a discussion, just like it was in a classroom, but when it came right down to it, the final decision was made by Mom. You always disappeared into you teaching and research."

"Maybe that's true," Charles admitted. "Some people like making decisions more than others. Your mother was always a very decisive person."

"You make it sound like it was easy for her. It wasn't. She even told me that she wished you'd do more of it."

"Did she really tell you that?"

Amy nodded. "More than once."

Charles sat there thinking about how one could be so wrong about a person you were so close to.

"I wonder why she didn't tell me?"

"She probably accepted that as being part of the way you were that would never change. I guess the good parts outweighed the bad parts. Isn't that always the way? After all, I like Jack's willingness to do the lion's share of the decision-making, and in exchange, I sometimes have to accept decisions I may not like."

"I don't think that sounds like a fair exchange. You're letting him run your life. Twenty years from now are you really going to be happy that instead of doing what you wanted to do, you did what he demanded you do."

"I don't know how I'll feel in twenty years, but right now, I'm pretty happy being a wife and mother. I know, I said yesterday that I might want more, but who doesn't have some dissatisfaction with their life."

Charles sighed. "Maybe I'm wrong, but yours sounds relatively major, sacrificing your chance to develop your abilities to their fullest."

"Maybe I'll get around to that at some time in the future."

"Do you think they'll ever be a time when Jack will give you permission to do that?"

"He's not a monster. If the time comes when I want it enough, he'll be happy for me to get a job."

"Just like his mother never did."

"Maybe she didn't want to."

"Maybe you should have a long talk with her some time and find out," Charles said, getting to his feet.

"So you are leaving?"

"It would be awkward to stay."

"Look, you and Jack are never going to be the best of friends, but for the sake of your grandsons, you both have to make an effort to get along. You only live a few hours away. You could visit much more frequently than you do."

Touched by the concern on Amy's face, Charles reached over and grasped her arm.

"I'll certainly make the effort. And I'm certain that Jack and I can reach a truce."

Amy nodded and smiled. "And don't worry. I am thinking about what is best for me."

"Make sure you do." Charles paused for a moment as an unrelated thought occurred to him. "From your time as a student at Opal, do you remember there being a faculty member with the name Marie?"

"Where did that question come from?"

"Just something I'm working on."

"Well, I didn't really know that faculty by their first names, except for the ones that were friends of yours. But I can't think of anyone named Marie."

Charles nodded. "Neither can I. But let me know if someone occurs to you."

He leaned over and gave Amy a kiss on the cheek, then went to the doorway and picked up his bag. Amy joined him there and gave him a hug.

"Make sure you come back soon, Dad."

"I will," he said, wondering if it was really true.

Chapter Thirty-Five

B y the time Charles got home, he was tired. It was a combination of the travel and not having slept well last night. As he walked from the garage to the front door, he realized that although he had only been away one day, it seemed much longer. He no longer felt anxious that someone might be out there with a rifle ready to shoot him. Although he was not realistically any safer, his time with Amy and the boys had broken the spell of fear that the shooting of the other night had put him under. But he still felt guilty about Karen.

He dropped his bag in the hall, and called Lieutenant Thorndike to find out about Karen's condition.

"It looks like she's going to be fine. They're keeping her in the hospital through tomorrow to run a few more tests, but then they should release her."

"I'd like to visit her if I could."

"I don't see why not. It might be best to see her during the day. She gets pretty tired by nighttime. How about tomorrow afternoon? I'm going to stop by myself then." Thorndike paused. "But I thought you were going to make yourself scarce for a few days."

"I spent yesterday at my daughter's, but I thought it was time to come home."

There was a delay that Charles figured was the Lieutenant trying to decide whether to ask any questions. She decided not to.

"Okay. But stay on the alert, especially when you're around your house. The shooter might set up outside somewhere waiting for you to come out."

"I'll be careful. Does Karen blame me for what happened?"

"I explained to her why I think she got shot. At first she was angry that you hadn't warned her about your situation, but I tried to make it clear to her that neither you nor I had taken the threat as seriously as we should have. I think she's pretty much forgiven you. She even said she was having a wonderful time until she got shot."

"Yeah, I can see where that might have put a damper on the evening."

"She seems to be a pretty good sport, and I think she really likes you."

Charles felt his heart sink. "I'm sorry to hear that."

"The feeling isn't mutual?"

"She's a very nice woman, but I don't think there's any chemistry there for me."

"Why did you go out with her, then?"

"She asked me, and I didn't know how to say no."

"Sometimes it's better to hurt someone a little, right away, when waiting means hurting the person worse."

"I know you're right."

"And that's the end of the lesson. Anything more from your friend at Yale."

"Not yet."

"Okay, well I'll see you tomorrow."

Charles immediately made two more calls. The first was to the woman in charge of the soup kitchen to let her know that he had come back early and would be there tomorrow. She sounded a bit surprised, but said she'd be happy to see him. He toyed with the idea of calling Greg Wasserman and arranging to run with him tomorrow morning, but finally decided that he would be putting Greg in a far too risky situation. If he really wanted to run, he could do so by himself.

Fortunately there was enough food in the house that he didn't have to go out again, so he curled up in the living room with the novel he'd started at Amy's and began to read. The phone rang, and this time it was Amy.

"I just wanted to check to see that you got home all right."

"No problems. And thanks again for putting me up for the night."

"Sorry it didn't go better. I just brought the boys home, and they're disappointed that grandpa isn't here."

Charles chuckled. "Tell them I'll be back to see them soon."

"I hope that turns out to be the case. Jack really shouldn't have made you feel so uncomfortable."

"I'm sure I disturbed him as much as he did me."

Amy was silent for a moment. "And you disturbed me, too."

"I'm sorry, Sweetheart, I should haves kept my opinions to myself."

173

"I think I needed to be disturbed. I'm like you in that I can get comfortable with the way things are and cruise along without considering whether they could be better. You've sort of broken down some psychological boundaries that I'd set for myself. Now I'm starting to see more opportunities."

"Just remember to take baby steps because you have to bring Jack along on this if you want your marriage to work."

"I know. I can be pretty good at compromise when I have to be."

"Let's hope Jack shares that skill," Charles said, although he had his doubts. He suspected that Jack was too much like his father to be malleable, but hoped he was wrong.

Charles hung up and sat back for a moment reflecting on Amy's situation. He certainly didn't want his interference to bring an end to her marriage. Barbara had always warned him not to express his reservations about Jack when he and Amy were first going out. She said the decision had to be Amy's. Charles had listened, but he'd never been convinced that his silence hadn't been a mistake. Jack had been head-over-heels in love with Amy, and Charles had always felt that Amy suffered from some of his inability to say no to those who are obviously taken with her. He thought of Lieutenant Thorndike's advice, and wondered if Amy shouldn't have broken the relationship off at the beginning when the disappointment would have been less severe.

Thinking of the Lieutenant, he recalled her question about his contact at Yale, and he decided it was time to give Adam Sussman a wake up call. He got right through to him.

"I was wondering if you'd had an opportunity to pursue that matter we spoke about," Charles said, knowing he sound like the stereotype of a secret agent.

"I've been working on it, Charles. The fly in the ointment has been that Christian Geller, the guy who I think would know the most, has been away for a few days. I finally managed to reach him, and we're scheduled to have lunch here in New Haven the day after tomorrow. It was the soonest he could see me."

"That sounds promising."

"It all depends on how much he knows. I think he'll be willing enough to talk to me and his memory seems great, but it will be a matter of how close he was to the scandal in the first place."

"Hopefully we'll end up knowing more than we do now."

"Do you really think Garrison's death traces back ten years to Yale?"

"If I'm wrong, then we really have no clue who the killer might be, and this person has already killed twice."

"Do you think he'd kill again?"

"If he had to in order to protect himself."

"I guess it always comes down to survival, doesn't it?"

"Yes," Charles said, thinking about the risk to his own life, "it definitely does."

• • • •

THE NEXT MORNING CHARLES waited until he was certain Greg would have left on his run, and then decided to go on his own. Just in case the shooter was waiting outside the front door, Charles went out the back. He quickly ran around the house, and went up the street zigzagging wildly from one side to the other to prevent a possible gunman from getting a good shot. He was sure that to anyone watching, he looked ridiculous, but as Adam had suggested, you did what you needed to do for self-survival.

He could easily imagine the shock of the bullet hitting his spine, tearing it apart. And he was only able to relax once he was over the hill and out of sight of home. At first he felt awkward, like his feet were hitting the ground too hard, and his glasses danced up and down on his nose. But soon his stride lengthened out, his muscles stretched, and he began to relax into a rhythm. This was the first that he had run by himself in over forty-five years, and he found it relaxing. Although he had appreciated having Greg along for silent encouragement, he had often found himself trying to match him stride for stride, which forced him into a faster pace than he was comfortable keeping. Having another person along was also a distraction to his mind, which wanted to go off on its own tangents before eventually coming into harmony with his body.

Sooner than he would have believed possible, Charles had reached the half-mile point. He was tempted to go farther, but recalled that he hadn't be able to make it quite all the way home the last time. Deciding he'd better keep something in the tank, he turned around and headed back. When he was about three blocks from home and still feeling pretty good, Charles began to put on speed, imagining he was in a race and could hear the roar of a cheering crowd.

Suddenly a car pulled up beside him. He glanced over as his heart rate jumped, half expecting to see the ugly muzzle of a revolver staring out at him.

"Charles," Andrea Boyd called out, "what are you doing?"

"Running," he managed to answer breathlessly.

"I can *see* that. But should you be out running when someone tied to shoot you at the movie theatre just the other night."

Charles stopped. "How do you know about that?"

Andrea brought the car to a halt. "One of your former students who's working on campus saw you there bending over the body. I just assumed because of what's been happening recently that the shot was meant for you. When I couldn't get you on your home phone yesterday and your cell went to voice mail, I got worried. I thought I'd stop by early and see how you were."

"Look, that's very nice of you, but could we talk about this back at my house."

"Sure. Do you want a ride?"

Charles gave the offer the look of contempt it deserved. "I'll meet you there."

As Charles ran the rest of the way, he realized that despite his dislike of being called on his cell phone, he should really turn it on more. Otherwise what was the point of having one?

He met Andrea in the driveway. They went into the house. He poured them each a cup of coffee. He offered her some cereal, but she said she'd already had breakfast. They sat down at the table and faced each other. She's studied him as if checking for hidden wounds.

"Are you sure you're all right?"

He nodded. "Why do you ask?"

"Well, I never thought you were one for physical exercise."

"I've picked up running since my retirement. I think I'm going to stay with it."

She nodded and sipped her coffee.

"So everyone at school knows I was involved in that shooting the other night?"

"There was an article in the *Opalsville Gazzett* about it. You weren't mentioned there. But your student's rumor has pretty much spread all around the school. Exactly what happened?"

Charles explained to her how his date had gone bad.

"And if she hadn't stepped in front of you, you would have been killed?"

Charles nodded, feeling a familiar shiver down his spine.

"The police think this ties in with Garrison's murder?"

"Right. They think whoever killed Garrison and his wife are behind the attempts on my life."

"But why?"

"Because I've been looking into the case. The police think I've gotten the killer worried, so now he's coming after me."

"What could you have done to make the killer nervous?"

"I've figured out that she must be someone who knew Garrison Underwood ten years ago at Yale. So I've been checking around to see who on campus was at Yale ten years ago. The only two people I found were Jessica Rhyser in theatre arts and Deborah Gould in biology. But they both claimed not to have known Underwood very well. Although it seemed to me that Gould might have been holding back something."

"Do you think one of them is the killer?"

Charles paused and stared across the kitchen.

"If I were to go by my intuition, I'd have to say no. Neither one of them liked Garrison from what they knew about him, but I didn't get the impression that they hated him enough to kill him. And now I've started to think that our killer may have left Yale and gotten her degree someplace else, so it could be any female faculty member in her thirties."

"But how do you know it was a woman from ten years ago?"

"There's this story running around Yale that he had some student as his sex slave. I figure she might have motive enough to kill him."

Andre shook her head in bewilderment. "Seems like quite a reach to me. From what I've heard about Garrison, he made enemies wherever he went, and he's probably gotten around a lot in the last ten years. And why would this woman you suspect have killed Sylvia Underwood."

"I've been giving that some thought, and I believe it was because Sylvia recognized her on campus. She was with Garrison at Yale, and may have known who this woman was. She probably hated her if she was Underwood's sex slave. When she saw her here at Opal, she would no doubt have taken her suspicions to the police."

"But you have no idea as to this woman's identity?"

He shook his head. "But I've got Adam Sussman looking into it. Do you remember Adam?"

She shook her head.

"Yeah, he might have graduated a year or two before you arrived. Well, he teaches at Yale now, and he's asking around to see if he can find out her identity."

"Ten years is a long time."

"Not so long at a place like Yale. People who get tenure tend to stay around. Somebody is bound to remember the Underwood case, and he or she just might remember the students involved."

Andrea reached across the table and put her hand on Charles' arm.

"Why don't you let this go, Charles? I don't want to lose one of my few friends on campus. This person has almost killed you three times. The fourth attempt might be the charm."

"I'm not going to do anything that raises any suspicions. I'll just go to the soup kitchen, check in at my office on campus, and keep in touch with the police to see if they've found out anything."

Andrea gave him a skeptical look. "Why does this not sound believable to me?"

"Oh, I may poke around a little, but not in any big way," he said smiling placidly.

Andrea got to her feet. "Well, I have to get back to work now. Scholarship waits for no woman."

"How's the article going?"

"I think I've broken the back of it. Now all I have to it wrap up my conclusion."

"I wish I felt that I was well on the way to wrapping up this case."

Charles stood up and Andrea gave him a hug. He hung onto her for a second longer than usual, enjoying the closeness of her presence.

"This isn't a substitute for that retirement dinner I promised you. We still have to get around to that."

"I'd like that," Charles said, as he walked her to the door.

Chapter Thirty-Six

Charles pulled into the parking lot at the soup kitchen. It have taken him an extra ten minutes to get there because he had followed a very circuitous route that allowed him to go on quiet streets where it was easy to check if he was being followed. Although he thought such safeguards were probably pointless since the killer knew where he lived and worked and could easily set up there and just wait for him, Charles decided that taking every precaution was probably prudent.

He went down the stairs to the cellar. A group of woman standing right outside the kitchen glanced up when he walked into the room. He said "hello" but was greeted with only curt nods and cold stares. Rachael had apparently told her version of events to everyone.

"I see you've had the courage to return," a voice said next to him.

He turned and saw Nancy, the woman in charge.

"You're not the most popular person around right now."

"I guess not," Charles said, watching the group of woman move away from him and reform on the other side of the room.

"From what I heard, you can't really blame them."

Charles shrugged. "There are two sides to every story, but I guess on either one of them I look pretty bad."

A smile played along Nancy's lips. "Well, at least you aren't trying to shirk blame. And it's good to have you back to help John set up the tables. I had to help him yesterday, and my back ached the whole night."

As if on cue, John came dancing across the floor doing his usual nervous fandango. Charles turned and walked to where the folded tables were leaning against the wall.

"What are you, some kind of gang banger?" John asked with a self-satisfied smiled.

"What are you talking about?"

"Well, those are the only guys I ever heard about who get shot during a drive-by shooting. Although I guess you were lucky and managed to hide behind a woman."

"It wasn't a drive-by and I wasn't hiding."

"Sure sounded like it to me. Most of the women threatened to quit if you came back."

"They still seem to be here."

"Nancy had to beg them to stay. Let's face it, you aren't a really popular guy."

"Do want to get started setting up the tables?" Charles said, shoving the first table in John's direction.

When the tables were all set up, Charles took his usual place at the serving table. He felt invisible. No one spoke to him or even continued a conversation when he was present. After his stint at serving was finished, he went into the kitchen where Rachel was wrestling with a large pot. He helped her carry it to the sink. She accepted his help without meeting his eye.

"Have you been to see Karen?" he asked.

"I saw her yesterday afternoon."

"How is she?"

Rachel gave him a glance as if he had a nerve to ask, but then relented. "She still has some pain, but she's going to be fine."

"I was planning to go see her today. Do you think she'd like that?"

"I have no idea," Rachel said, setting her mouth in a firm line.

"Did she say anything about me?"

"I didn't ask."

"Well, thanks for the information," Charles said, purposely kept any hint of sarcasm out of his voice. Rachel had a right to be angry, although a bit more understanding might not have been out of line.

He checked his watch. It was just after one, when visiting hours began. So he decided to head right over to the hospital and get the chore over with. He didn't expect Karen to forgive him—that wasn't the point—he had to apologize because he had done something wrong. The least he could have done was explain to her that there might be some risk in associating with him. Even though he hadn't thought there was much risk, he should have made her ware of the possibility and allowed her to decide for herself. Instead he had deceived her into thinking she was safe. He decided to stop off on the way for a bouquet of flowers.

The hospital was rather small for the purpose, nestled into a grove of pine trees and looking more like a small resort than a medical facility. Charles walked thorough the front doors into a lobby and up to the circular front desk. He asked for Karen Melrose's room and was directed to go to his right and look for room forty-seven. He walked down the stylishly tiled hall. The walls were covered with paintings that must have been by local artists because each carried a sale price. He wondered who bought paintings off a hospital wall. Charles was still musing over the connections between capitalism and medical care when he reached Karen's room. After a momentary pause to brace himself for what might come, he pushed open the door.

The first thing he saw was Karen sitting up in bed, looking much the same as when he had seen her last except for an obvious bandage on her right shoulder, which was in a sling.

"Charles," she said, reaching out with her left hand, "how good of you to have come."

Charles took her hand. On the other side of the bed stood a woman in her thirties who was staring at him fiercely, and he was aware of a man of approximately the same age at the foot of the bed who also seemed less than pleased to see him. In the corner Lieutenant Thorndike looked on with a neutral expression.

"It was the least I could do," he said, handing her the flowers.

"Oh, aren't they lovely, Angie," Karen said, handing them to the young woman, who stared at them as though they were weeds.

"It certainly is the least you could do," the young man said, coming around the bed toward Charles. Short and rather willowy, Charles didn't feel he posed much of a physical threat. "We're going to sue you. Then you'll find out how much you have to do for getting my mother shot."

"We'll do not such thing," Karen said sharply.

"Aww, Ma," the young man said. "He deserves to pay."

"He didn't shoot me. He was almost killed himself. And I was having a marvelous time until I got shot." She looked at Charles affectionately. "As you may have gathered, these are my children: Angie, the dentist, and Roger, the lawyer.

Angie looked at him like she was awaiting the opportunity to drill his teeth down to the roots, and Roger was still chomping at the maternal bit holding him back from litigation.

"Hello," Charles said, smiling, and not being surprised when he got none in return.

"Now, I'd like to have a moment alone with Charles if you wouldn't mind," Karen said.

Her children looked at her in amazement as if she had just asked them to leave her alone with a serial killer. The Lieutenant stood up first. She waited for the children to leave in front of her. As she closed the door behind her, she gave Charles a quick wink.

When the room was empty, Karen once again took Charles's hand and looked up at him.

"I have no intention of letting my children punish you in any way for what happened. As Lieutenant Thorndike has explained to me, you have no reason to believe that you life was in quite such imminent danger. If you had been more aware of the situation, I'm sure you would never have exposed me to such risk."

She looked inquisitively at Charles, who nodded solemnly.

"All that being said, however, I'm afraid we're going to have to break up."

Charles looked surprised, mostly at the thought that they had ever been together, but Karen took it as a sign of shocked dismay.

"Please don't be upset, Charles. It isn't that I don't like you, but the life you live is obviously much more adventurous than mine. You're a very brave person who clearly is not afraid of risk, while I'm inclined to want safety and security. I know we have a certain chemistry, but that isn't enough to overcome our basic differences in our approach to life."

"So you're dumping me," Charles said, using a blunt expression so everything would be absolutely clear.

"Yes," she replied.

She had tears in her eyes as Charles struggled to keep the smile from his face. She must have taken that for an effort to control deep emotions.

"Don't feel too badly, Charles," she said taking his hand and giving it a hard squeeze. "We'll still get to see each other at the soup kitchen. We can still be friends and stay in each other's lives."

"Of course, of course," Charles intoned. "Thank you for letting me down so gently."

He was afraid he might be going too far, but her radiant smile told him he had been right on target.

"I wouldn't hurt your feeling for the world," she said. Then she gave an abrupt nod of her head. "I guess it's time to let my children back in the room."

"I'll get them," Charles said, moving toward the door. "Get well quickly, Karen, and I'll see you at the soup kitchen."

She gave him a smile and a wave. He went out into the hall. Angie and Roger were standing right across from him, looking as if only the Lieutenant's presence right next to the door kept them from attacking Charles.

"Nice meeting you," he said, getting no response.

The children walked past him and back into the room. He walked down the hall with the Lieutenant beside him.

"Thanks for being there," he said.

"I didn't really think a violent confrontation would break out, but it's never good to have disorderly conduct in a hospital. But Karen seemed to handle it well."

"She dumped me," Charles said, realizing he sounded sadder than he felt. He wondered if he actually was sad. It was the first time a girl had broken up with him since college, and suddenly he wasn't quite sure how he felt.

"I'm sorry."

"Don't be. It wouldn't have worked out. I think I'm the kind of guy destined to only have one love in his life."

"Your wife must have been a very special woman."

He nodded. "And thank you for explaining to Karen about why I didn't think I was in real danger."

Thorndike shrugged. "That was as much my fault as yours. I should have been more alarmed by the rat incident. But for the time being keep a low profile. We don't want to encourage any more attacks on your life."

"Stay in touch," Charles said as they parted in the parking lot.

Thorndike smiled. "Don't worry, I will."

Chapter Thirty-Seven

T he next morning, Charles went out for his run. Again he took the precaution of leaving from the back door and zigzagging his way up the street. Two days had passed since the last attempt on his life, and he found himself feeling more optimistic about his chances of survival. He thought about how irrational optimism could sometimes be, and considered how evolution had probably selected for optimism as a positive trait. Those cavemen who despaired at the prospect of struggling for another day probably didn't have many offspring, while those who figured the saber-toothed tiger would never catch them and looked forward to dining on Mammoth burger the next evening were more inclined to procreate.

Considering these thoughts, Charles was past the half-mile mark almost before he realized it. He went a few blocks more just to show he could, then turned around and made his way back home, running at a steady pace the whole way. At this rate, he congratulated himself, he'd be able to keep up with Greg once they started running together again after all this was over. Some of his optimism left him when he considered that if the murder or murders were never caught, he'd be looking over his shoulder for the rest of his life. Although he had confidence in the Lieutenant, he hoped that he heard from Adam soon and that the information was helpful.

After pacing in his backyard for a few minutes to cool down, he went in the back door.

He went into the kitchen and poured himself a cup of coffee. As he sat at the table, he began to consider whether there was anything more he could do to help solve the crimes. He reviewed all the events that had happened so far, and the one issue that stuck out in his mind was Deborah Gould's apparent hesitance to be completely open with him. Could her relationship with Underwood ten years ago have gone beyond that of a teacher and student? She hadn't struck Charles as being a killer, but there had been a suspicious reticence about her. The Lieutenant had sensed the same thing. Charles decided that another conversation with her might be in order. It would be a breech of his promise to both the Lieutenant and

Amy not to stay involved in the case, but he didn't think he'd be in much danger on campus. The attempts on his life and all been carefully staged, and it would be impossible for the killer to predict where he would be going once he went to the College. And even if there was some risk, he strongly felt this case had to be solved quickly.

After having his breakfast, he dressed, putting on a sport shirt and a pair of chinos. No more tie and sport coat now that he was retired, he thought. It was time for a new and more casual life style. He took his new and circuitous route to school that allowed him to check whether he was being followed, and he even pulled into another parking lot a distance away from the English building. That should avoid his ending up with another rodent companion.

As had become customary since the murders, there were more campus security people walking around the campus and standing by some of the larger building. There was no one stationed in front of the science building, but a newly posted sign said that anyone wishing entry had to swipe his or her ID card. Charles recalled that the previous rule had only required that this be done after six o'clock and on weekends. Obviously security had been tightened. Fortunately Charles had his ID card with him. Like many educational institutions that are strict in theory but loose in practice, there had been no requirement that he turn in his card, probably because he occupied a twilight area of still being a peripheral part of the institution.

He swiped his card and heard the dull metallic click of the door lock being released. He slowly pushed it open and went inside the shadowy hall. He went to the bottom of the stairwell and began climbing his long way up to the third floor. Like most buildings built in the nineteenth century, it had not been designed with an elevator. Charles thought it likely that one had been added for disabled students, but it would probably be in a hard to find spot. With his new and improved conditioning, he was certain that four floors would not be a challenge. He discovered that although his breathing was fine, by the time he reached the fourth floor the muscles in his legs had tightened into hard rocks. He decided that he would have to add more hills to his running routine.

He walked down the dark hall to the biology lab. He pushed open the door and saw that it was dark inside. Clearly Deborah

185

wasn't working there today. He had decided to go one floor down and check at her office when on a whim he switched on the lights in the lab. He didn't know exactly why. Certainly Gould wouldn't be working in the dark. Everything looked as was to be expected. There were rows of benches with high stools lined up in front of them. He stepped into the room and slowly made his way down to where Deborah had been working the last time he was there. He remembered how startled she had been at his arrival, and how the slide had flipped out of her hand and had barely been caught by him.

He would never have noticed if he hadn't taken one final step forward, but something white on the floor caught his eye. He moved forward quickly then suddenly stopped, listening to his accelerating heartbeat. Deborah was lying on the floor, her white lab coat dark crimson blood, underneath her lay a large viscous pool of blood. There was nothing lifelike about her face, which looked stiff and frozen, her eyes blank.

Charles turned and walked away from the scene. When he reached the door to the lab he stopped, took out his cell phone, and dialed 9-1-1. He was pleased to see that his hand barely shook as he gave the responder his information.

• • • •

THE LIEUTENANT SAT across from him in the police interview room that was beginning to feel like his home away from home. A tepid cup of coffee sat in front of him that Thorndike had already apologized about more than once. He could tell by her expression that she was extremely unhappy. He hoped it was because of another person being killed and not with him. When she began to speak, he realized it was both.

"What are we going to do with you, Charles? You keep finding dead bodies wherever you go."

He shrugged and gave a small smile.

"It's not like I go looking for them."

"Not exactly. But if you had stayed out of this investigation, as you promised me the last time we talked, at least you wouldn't have been the one to find this body."

Somebody had to find it, better sooner than later, he thought, but decided the comment should be kept to himself.

"She looked very dead," he said, hoping the comment wouldn't be considered as absurd as it sounded.

"The preliminary medical examination estimates that she had been dead eighteen to twenty-four hours before you found her."

"She died yesterday afternoon. Why didn't anyone find her body sooner than that?"

"Apparently no one used the lab in that period of time. The lights were out and security doesn't go through each room. They just go up and down the halls."

"How did she die?"

"Shot through the heart, just like Sylvia Underwood."

"So probably the same killer."

"Like I've said before Charles, I think it's unlikely that we have multiple murderers using the same method in a place the size of Opalsville. What were you doing in the lab?"

"I went there to talk to Gould because I thought she was holding back the last time I questioned her." The bland look the Lieutenant gave him provoked him to add. "You thought the same thing after questioning her."

"Yes, I did. You should have mentioned your doubts to me the last time we talked, and I would have spoken to her again. I'd have been more likely to get more information out of her than you would have."

"I only thought of it this morning. By then she was already dead."

Charles sat there, knowing he looked sullen. But he didn't think he deserved to be accused of doing something wrong, and he was disappointed that once again the killer had been a step ahead of him.

The Lieutenant face brightening. "I can actually think of a way your interest in this investigation can help me. I have Jessica Rhyser in a room down the hall. It might be helpful if you could talk to her with me."

"You want me to sit in on an interview?" Charles said, feeling his interest rise.

"You know her and have generally the same work background. You also found the body. She may be more open to talking to you. You can take the lead."

Charles agreed and the Lieutenant led him down the hall. When he entered the interview room, he immediately noticed that Jessica's face was swollen and her eyes red as if she had been crying.

"I'm sorry about Deborah's death. I know the two of you were good friends," Charles said.

Jessica nodded. "I just don't understand why anyone would do this to her."

Charles cleared his throat and said slowly, "We think it may have something to do with Garrison Underwood's death."

"Deborah hardly knew Underwood. She had him for a semester of English, but that's all the contact they had. I knew more about him than she did." She pause and her eyes widened. "Do you think the same killer is after me?"

"We don't think so," the Lieutenant said. "But we'll assign a police officer to keep an eye on you just in case."

"When I talked to Deborah, I got the impression that she might have known more about Underwood than she was telling me. Do you think that's possible?"

The woman shook her head. "I'm certain she told me everything about him that she knew. We used to talk about it a lot and laugh over it. We would even play a game where we would try to guess what male faculty member at Opal College was most likely to get into the same kind of trouble."

"I hope my name never came up," Charles said.

Jessica laughed. "It was never mentioned."

Charles didn't now whether to be flattered or insulted.

"Was there anything unusual or mysterious that she said to you recently?" Charles asked.

Jessica paused, then she slowly nodded. "The other day, right after Underwood was killed, we had lunch together. We were speculating over who might have wanted to murder him." She looked directly at Charles. "Your name did come up then."

"I'm sure."

"Not that we really thought you'd done it."

"That's a relief."

"Anyway, Deborah got real quiet, and then she said that there was one person who might have had more reason than most."

"Did she tell you who it was?" asked the Lieutenant.

188

Jessica shook her head. "I asked, but she said she'd promised the person that she wouldn't tell. All she would say is that it was someone she had met at Yale."

"Is it someone who teaches here?" Charles asked.

"I asked her that, but she wouldn't tell me."

"Was there anything she said that might have given you a hint as to the person's identity?' the Lieutenant pressed.

"When Deborah told me that she had promised this person not to tell, she said, 'She'd be very disappointed in me if I broke my promise.' So I figured it was a woman."

When it was clear that Jessica Rhyser knew nothing more, The Lieutenant thanked her and let her go. Then she sat back down at the interview table and stared at Charles.

"Any new ideas," she asked.

"Just that the list is narrowing down. Even if they didn't have solid alibis, which they do, we can eliminate Ernest Ritter and Greg Wasserman."

"More importantly, we can also eliminate Nora Chapman. It sounds like this mystery person was someone Deborah had known for a while, and I doubt she ever even met Nora."

"So we have no suspects left except for this mystery woman."

"Who appears to go back to Underwood's days at Yale like you suspected all along. That was a good hunch."

Pleased by Thorndike's compliment, Charles tried to look modest.

"I could easily have been wrong," he said.

"Now all we have to do is discover her identity. I take it you haven't heard anything from your friend down at Yale."

"He's still working on it."

"Maybe I should contact the New Haven police department and see if one of their detectives would accompany me to Yale. If I interviewed their English faculty myself, I might be able to find out something sooner."

"Possibly. But it's summer. Probably their faculty is spread all over the world, either relaxing or doing scholarly things. You might only get to interview a small fraction of them."

"It only takes the right one. How many female members do you have in the English Department at Opal?"

"If you count the part-timers probably five or six. And how many of them are the right age to have been at Yale a decade ago."

Charles thought for a long moment. "Probably four."

"And as far as you know, none of them went to Yale."

He shook his head.

"If Yale doesn't pan out, I'll start by interviewing them. Four is a manageable number."

"But it could be someone from another department. I doubt that Underwood confined his attentions to women in one discipline."

The Lieutenant frowned. "We have to begin somewhere. If those four don't work out, we'll expand our parameters to include the whole female faculty of the right age. This person went to Yale for a while, and you can't hide your academic background forever."

Charles nodded, but he was thinking about the Ukrainian physics professor who had hidden his lack of a PhD for over ten years. The College had only checked his credentials after someone at a conference remarked to another member of the Opal physics department that Georg had never finished his dissertation. Georg had quickly been banished back to the Ukraine. Charles had always felt sorry for him because the man had a reputation as an excellent teacher.

The Lieutenant stood up. "Keep after your contact at Yale. That may be our big break. And be careful, especially if you notice any women acting strangely around you."

"Women don't usually pay much attention to me."

"What about Karen Melrose?" Thorndike said with a grin.

Charles smiled back. "She's not young enough to be the killer, and I doubt she's been to Yale."

"Did you ever ask her about her education?"

Charles realized with surprise that he never had. He wondered if it was due to an assumption that she had never been to college or at least not to a very good one. She had never mentioned anything about her past aside from being a widow and being the mother of two. And he had never tried to go beyond that. Had he been fooling himself all these years into thinking that he was a great democrat, able to relate to people from all walks of life, while in reality he was as much of an elitist as his father? Did he only pay real attention to people who had a similar education to his own?

He promised himself that if he ever went out again, he'd ask the woman more questions about herself.

"So we'll leave it at that for now, Charles," the Lieutenant said, stepping aside to let him precede her out the door. When they reached the lobby she put her hand on his arm. The warmth of her hand felt soothing and intimate. "Stay in touch, Charles."

He remembered that it was a direct reversal of their conversation the last time they had parted.

"Don't worry, I will," he promised.

Chapter Thirty-Eight

After driving home, Charles had a late lunch, and then went to sit in his study. He sat behind his desk where he had spent so much time remembering the past and imagining what the future might have been in the years since Barbara's death. He tried to slip back into that frame of mind, so comfortable in its darkness and despondency, like a worn shoe where every rub and pinch had a sort of fond familiarity. But he found that his mind wouldn't go there. It stubbornly kept returning to the question of who had killed Underwood. Would it remain unsolved just like the other great mystery of his life? What had put Barbara on the road so late on that snowy night? Would these two unanswered questions nag him into his old age, preoccupying his thoughts whenever he wasn't caught up in the mundane decisions of life?

He made an effort to pull himself back from the brink of hopelessness. The mystery of who killed Underwood was still likely to be solved. Since it was most likely someone at the College, it would be a person he knew. Charles reviewed in his mind all the female faculty of the proper age, but couldn't see any of them as being capable of killing three people. Of course, he reminded himself, the Lieutenant would doubtlessly warn him that appearances sometimes tell you nothing. Still, he wondered, perhaps the woman was someone Deborah had known from off campus. Even in Opalsville, the division between town and gown wasn't a hermetic seal. And it was always possible that someone who had gone to Yale had located in the town and never had any direct connection with the College. Especially in these days of Internet access, a bright ivy-league grad might live in Opalsville and be able to work on a challenging job somewhere else in the world.

Frustrated by his inability to gain any traction in solving this mystery, Charles picked up his landline phone and called Adam Sussman. Both his office phone and cell took Charles to voice mail. He chose not to leave a message, not wanting to take on the role of the retired professor who expected others to devote all their time to his hobbyhorse. He could imagine Adam, even now, free of the telephone, beavering away on some project that would bring him academic fame and tenure. Charles reflected on that time in his life. All the energy he had given when young had provided himself and Barbara with a comfortable, satisfying life, and he freely admitted to having enjoyed the fame he had gained even if it was in a rather circumscribed arena. He could still understand Adam's motivation, but it was no longer there for him, at least not in the world of scholarship. The most alive he had felt since his wife's death had been in the days since the murder of Underwood. Perhaps it was shucking off the old job that had long ago outlived its ability to inspire, but perhaps more importantly had been the desire to solve a new mystery. One that involved life and death rather than scholarly details.

Deciding that he had engaged in enough introspection for one afternoon, he got up from his desk and went into the living room. He sat in his easy chair and picked up the latest novel he was working on. But in a few moments, he was asleep.

The next morning, after his run and breakfast, he spent an hour cleaning the downstairs of the house. He usually did the downstairs twice a week and the upstairs once a week on a schedule that he had adhered to since Barbara's death. But since Underwood's death and his sudden retirement, he hadn't touched the place. The recent changes in his life seemed to have shattered all the old routines. He wondered whether, if the Underwood murder were solved, he would quickly return to his previous patterns. He rather hoped not. His old way of life simply would not be enough to sustain him now that he was no longer working, and he would need more than the soup kitchen to keep him busy. Thinking of the soup kitchen, he realized that it was his day to work. With more than a little dread, he recalled the almost public shunning he had experience the last time he was there. He could only hope that as Karen recovered and her return to good health became known, her friends would be a bit less harsh in their judgment of him.

Finishing up his chores, he got in the car and drove his now normal secured route to the soup kitchen. When he got out of his car, a woman whose name he didn't remember was carrying garbage out to the dumpster. Not expecting any recognition, he looked away and was surprised when she called out his name and waved.

Once he was down in the cellar, several other women unexpectedly smiled at him. Those who'd had nothing but frowns for him yesterday seemed happy to see him. It wasn't long before he found out why. Sitting in the middle of the work area in a large chair that looked for all-the- world like a small throne, sat Karen. Although her injured arm was still in a sling, she used her other arm to gesture enthusiastically to those who were gathered around her liked court attendants. Charles glanced around the room looking for John, so they could get started setting up the tables, but he was nowhere in sight. Before he could search for him, he heard Karen call his name. A he walked toward her the other women disappeared, returning to their jobs, as if to give them a moment of privacy.

"It's good to see you looking so well," Charles said.

"I'm on pain medication up to the gills," Karen whispered. "But don't worry it's only over-the-counter stuff," she said, seeing Charles' worried expression. "And I think it hurts a little less every day."

"But should you be here?"

Karen nodded firmly. "I talked to Rachel last night, and I finally got her to understand that what happened to me really wasn't your fault. Then she told me how the other people had been treating you, and I realized that the only way to set things right was for me to come here and talk to them personally. I think things will be all right for you here now."

"Thanks, Karen, I really appreciate it. If there's anything I can do . . ."

"I'll be just fine between my family and my friends, and I meant what I said yesterday about our relationship," she said, giving Charles a stern look. "Nothing more than friends."

Putting a disappointed expression on his face, he nodded.

"But once I'm my feet so to speak, we an get back to working next to each other again."

"I'll look forward to it."

"There you are," a voice said, and John clapped him on the back like they were old friends. "No more time for talking. We have to get these tables set up."

A bit stunned by the turn around in things, Charles went about doing his tasks, wondering how Karen could possibly have changes people's mind so quickly. It wasn't until he went into the kitchen towards the end of the meal where Rachel was working on a pot larger than herself that he understood.

Rachel motioned him over.

"I don't know if you've heard, but Karen is telling people that you tried to throw yourself between her and the bullet the other night. That what you did probably saved her life."

"That isn't true."

"I *know* that. I was *there*. But Karen has built up this whole romantic version of events where you had tears in your eyes as you gently placed her down on the ground and told her that you loved her."

"That didn't exactly happen either."

Rachel let out a disgusted puff of air to blow some hair off of her forehead.

"Of course it isn't. But the least you can do is go along with it. Karen needs to remember things this way in order to carry on, so we aren't going to disabuse her. Got it."

Charles looked down at the diminutive woman who was staring up at him so fiercely.

"Got it," he replied.

"Good. Things will go easier on you this way, too. But remember I know the truth, and I think you were a heel."

Charles still thought that judgment was a bit harsh, but decided not to argue the point. He nodded, then turned and left the kitchen.

When he got back to the serving area a crowd of women were following Karen outside as she slowly walked across the parking lot to a waiting car. Charles joined them, and quickly found himself at the front of the procession next to Karen. As they reached the car, he saw that her son was on the driver's side. He gave Charles a look that said he would still like to have his day in court. Ignoring him, Charles gallantly opened the passenger door for Karen, and fussed rather ineffectually as she managed to get into the seat with the use of only one arm. She leaned out the window and addressed those gathered.

"I should be back to working with you all in a couple of weeks if the healing goes as expected. Please come to visit me if you get a chance, I'd like to know what's going on." She gave the crowd a final gracious wave as her son slowly pulled away.

Charles walked back to his car thinking about how stories were always subject to a variety of interpretations. There were some theorists that would even argue that there were only interpretations and no such thing as truth. Charles had always felt that view was wrong and that there was a standard of truth by which various versions could be measured. He was sure that Karen's story was quite far from the facts, even though it made her happy. He also thought, partially for his own peace of mind, that Rachel's understanding of what happened was also not quite accurate. But where did you turn for the truth then. Was he simply going to say by fiat that his account of events was true for him so true for everyone? With all these thought whirling around in his head, he got in his car and drove toward the College.

Chapter Thirty-Nine

As Charles walked across the parking lot to the rear of the English Building, the door opened and Ernest Ritter walked out. In his tight fitting black suit and prancing walk, he reminded Charles for all the world of some concertmaster in a minor eighteenth century German principality: a big fish in a little pond and proud of it.

Ritter stopped to confront Charles.

"What are you doing here? I thought you were retired," he asked suspiciously.

"Don't worry, Ernest, I'm not here to take back my courses. I just had a bit of business to conduct."

"Well, I've spent the morning in my office trying to straighten out your 17th to 18th Survey of American Literature. "Your syllabus was hopelessly out of date. You spend far too much time on the Transcendentalists and not enough on Whitman. No one reads the poetry of Emerson anymore."

"Perhaps they should. Anyway, it's your course now, so you are free to structure it as you wish."

"Has there been any progress in discovering who killed Underwood?"

Charles shook his head.

Ritter smiled maliciously. "Do they still suspect you?"

"I think I'm safely out of the picture."

Charles thought again how pleasant it would be if Ritter were charged with the murder. Unfortunately he had been elsewhere rather than his office at the time of Underwood's death. He office was right above Charles', so even if he had been there that day he wouldn't have had to pass Charles' office to come and go. Therefore, he wouldn't have been even a useful witness.

"I'm surprised. Especially since you were also on the scene when Sylvia Underwood was killed. And didn't you also find poor Deborah Gould's body yesterday?"

"I'm unlucky, not culpable."

Ritter laughed. "Sounds like you've been talking with a lawyer."

"I haven't felt the need so far, Ernest."

Ritter gave him a level stare. "Perhaps you should reconsider."

Giving him a curt nod, Charles walked into the English Building and up the stairs to his office. Instead of going in, he walked several doors down and entered the English Department Office. The secretary looked up from her work and gave him a sympathetic smile.

"How are *you*? It must have been terrible finding Deborah Gould like that. Do the police have any leads on who did it?"

"Nothing very definite," he replied. Not wanting to get pulled into a lengthy discussion of the murder, he turned toward his mailbox. Since his retirement was so new, it was full of mail, most of it no longer important to him. He threw a handful of it in the wastebasket. He was relieved to see that the near shooting the other night hadn't made it everywhere onto the College grapevine.

Yuri came out of his office and approached Charles.

"Ah, Charles, such sorrowful times. To have not one, or two, but three murders on campus within a week is most stressful."

"Yes, it certainly doesn't help the reputation of the college."

"Indeed, Dean Caruthers was about to have puppies yesterday when he heard about Professor Gould's death."

"I believe the expression is 'have kittens,'" Charles corrected.

Looking stricken, Yuri fumbled a notebook out of his shirt pocket and made himself a note.

"He was very distressed," Yuri continued, safely staying away for colloquialisms.

"That's understandable. Parents become nervous when they hear about crime on the campus where they are sending their sons and daughters to live."

"I've heard rumors that the admissions office has received several phone calls from parents who wish to withdraw their children from this fall's entering class."

Charles nodded and tried to look concerned, although he really felt the problem was no longer his own.

"I met Ernest in the parking lot. He seems to be working hard at adapting my survey course."

Yuri rolled his eyes. "I dread to think how many students will be in my office by the middle of next semester complaining about the low grades he's giving them. The man seems to think that low grades are proof of good teaching. I think it is just the opposite. The man can't teach, and he blames the students for not learning. I'd like to give all your classes to Andrea Boyd, but the Dean won't let me. He says we need a tenured person teaching some of them. But Ritter, I tell you, the man is a mule."

Charles thought he meant ass, but didn't correct him. Tiring of the conversation, he edged away from Yuri.

"Well, maybe once the Dean sees how hopeless Ritter is, he'll change his mind."

Yuri nodded doubtfully. "But if you ever want to teach part-time, one course a semester, I'm certain I could get the Dean to go along."

"I appreciate the offer, Yuri, but I think teaching and I have permanently parted."

"Never say never," Yuri intoned. "After all, you don't want to build your bridges behind you."

"I think that's 'burn your bridges,'" Charles said, and slipped away while Yuri was getting out his notebook.

Charles walked down the hall and unlocked the door to his office. The room smelled a bit musty, but the temperature was comfortable. Fortunately, during the last plant improvement campaign central air conditioning had been installed throughout the building. Generally he enjoyed the increased comfort, but Charles still remembered with some longing the long summer days he had worked in this office with the smells of summers wafting off the hills and in through his open window. Somehow he felt more in touch with the nineteenth century when he didn't have all the creature comforts of the twenty-first.

He settled behind his desk and thought for amount about what to do next. He reached over and picked up his desk phone and tapped in the code that gave him his voice mail. Nothing. He checked his watch. Adam had been meeting with his source over lunch today. The fact that he hadn't already called didn't bode well. Perhaps the man had provided no relevant information. Not willing to waste more time in idle speculation, Charles picked up the phone and punched in Adam's number.

"Hello," Adam answered, sounding distracted.

"This is Charles Bentley, sorry to disturb you."

"Oh, yes, Charles. Sorry I didn't get back to you sooner. But I woke up this morning with a completely new take on how to approach this article I'm doing, and I wanted to get right on it after lunch."

"You have to strike while the creative juices are running," Charles said, suspecting he'd jumbled his metaphors. "Did you learn anything from luncheon guest today?"

There was a long pause while Adam seemed to be searching for the thread of the conversation.

"I believe you were having lunch with Christian Geller."

"Of course, what a charming old boy."

"Did he have any information to add about the Underwood scandal," Charles asked a shade impatiently.

Adam's voice came closer to the phone and he sounded more focused when he said, "He couldn't remember the name of the female student who was most involved. He thought her name was Marie something. But he did remember that after the scandal broke she left to go to school in California."

"Is that all you learned?" Charles asked, disappointed.

"Yes, sorry. Apparently only senior people were involved in the proceedings, and all of them are either dead or retired. I supposed I could get the names of those who retired and give them a call. However, they'd probably be reluctant to talk to me about something of a disciplinary nature. Confidentiality is emphasized a lot today as you know."

Charles sighed. "Well, thank you for looking into things."

"No problem. Let me know if you ever get it all figured out."

"That's a promise. And maybe we can get together if you get up here for an alumni event."

"I'll plan on it."

After hanging up with Adam, Charles gave the Lieutenant a call and reported what he had learned.

"The name Marie again. And there's no Marie on the faculty," said Thorndike.

"Correct. The only Marie was in personnel, and she certainly wasn't the one."

Charles remembered with a blush his experience there.

"It stands to reason the woman might have changed her name if she stayed in the field," Thorndike said. "People tend to know each other in English literature, don't they?"

"Well, there are a lot of people teaching college English, but when you get to the more elite levels like Opal and Yale, people would know each other from conferences and publications. If you want to be successful, it's hard to remain anonymous. So she might have changed her name. But it doesn't matter, we don't have a last name anyhow."

"How about female English faculty of the right age who got their degrees from California universities?"

"I know where everyone in the English Department went, and none of them are from schools in California."

A sound of exasperation came down the line. "I think this person has put some effort into concealing her background."

"Maybe, maybe not. When there's a disciplinary action involving a faculty member and a student, the school would try very hard to keep the student's name confidential. When she left Yale, she could have wandered around for a while, sometimes graduate students do that."

"Maybe I'll go down to New Haven and have a chat with this Adam Sussman. See if he has any more ideas about who I could talk to. I might even try contacting retired members of the disciplinary board. This is a murder case after all, and there are limits to academic confidentiality."

"It's worth a try. I'm afraid I'm out of ideas. I'd hoped for more from Adam."

"Probably its for the best that you stay out of the investigation from now on. Remember, someone is still gunning for you. A low profile might be the safest."

"I suppose you're right."

"I'll let you know if I turn up anything."

"Thanks."

After hanging up, Charles sat behind his desk feeling thoroughly disappointed. Just like the question of why Barbara had been on that snowy road at night had remained unanswered, so the matter of Underwood's death was threatening to become another mystery that would continue to haunt him. When the Lieutenant had asked him whether any of the female English faculty had gone to school in California, a name had bounced around at the edge of his memory. He started up his computer and went to the faculty listing that gave people's degrees. He had been right, no one in English had listed a degree from a California school. Just to be diligent, he checked the entire faculty roster. Aside from one fellow in science and another man in history, there were no other degrees listed as coming from California. Opal tended to favor those with eastern degrees.

Charles wondered if there was anyone else who might know if someone had studied out there. He went out into the hall and looked in the direction of Andrea's office. The door was open, so he wandered down the hall and looked inside. She was sitting behind her desk working busily on the computer and didn't see him in the doorway until he cleared his throat.

"Hello, Charles, you seem to spend as much time on campus now as before you retired," she said, turning away from the screen.

"I'm gradually weaning myself off of academic life. A sudden withdrawal might be too much for me," he said, settling into the chair in front of her desk.

"That's probably wise."

"The reason I stopped by is that I was wondering if you knew of any female faculty member who went to school in California. Adam Sussman said that the women involved with Underwood at Yale went out to California after the incident. Her first name was Marie."

Andrea stared into space. "I don't know anyone on the faculty here named Marie. I'm trying to think if anyone went to school on the west coast."

"I checked the faculty roster. There are only two male faculty who list degrees from out there."

Andrea gave him a sad smile. "I'm afraid I can't help you, then. But let me repeat what I asked you last time, is it really so important that you find out who killed Underwood? He doesn't sound like very much of a loss to me."

Charles nodded. "I only met the man for a few minutes, and I disliked him intensely. I'm certainly not doing it for him. But I want to know." He paused, not sure how much he wanted to reveal himself to Andrea. "You know that night Barbara died, she was late getting home from work. There was never any explanation as to why she didn't arrive home two hours earlier. Well, that's been bothering me ever since. And I just don't have the room for two mysteries in my life."

He was about to go on when his cell phone rang. He excused himself and answered.

202

"Hi, Dad," Amy said.

"Hello, Sweetheart, I'm in Andrea's office right now. Was there anything you wanted to tell me?"

Amy hesitated. "Well, you asked me if I knew of any faculty members named Marie. It just came to me yesterday that Mom once mentioned to me that she and Andrea had the same middle name: Marie."

Charles struggled to keep his face blank.

"Okay, Amy, thanks for the information. But I guess it doesn't matter anymore. Remember, I love you."

Without giving her a chance to respond, he cut the connection. He sat staring at the floor for a moment as a memory came rushing back to him. It was also something Barbara had said about Andrea one night just before they went to sleep. She mentioned that Andrea had commented on how conservative Berkeley had seemed when she was there as compared to what she had heard about it in the sixties.

Charles looked up. Andrea still sat behind her desk, but now she had a gun pointing at the middle of his chest.

"I'm afraid your face is an open book, Charles. It always has been."

Charles shrugged. "I'm afraid I can't say the same about yours."

She smiled. "I've learned over the years to be a bit opaque."

"How did you ever end up getting intimately involved with Garrison Underwood in the first place?"

"You thought I'd have better taste?"

Charles nodded, never taking his eyes off of the gun.

"It was blackmail pure and simple. I had Underwood for a graduate class. I wrote a paper for the class, and I really wanted to impress him. I came across this really obscure book on the Romantic Movement in England and took one of its theses for my own. I figured no one else would be aware of the book. It looked like it hadn't been read in fifty years."

"So you took the idea without attribution?"

"Not a footnote in sight. I know, the cardinal sin of scholarship. Unfortunately, for reasons I was never clear on, Underwood had read the book and remembered the ideas. He threatened me with expulsion for plagiarism if I didn't have sex with him. What choice did I have?"

"Are you sure you really didn't want to?"

203

"Don't be silly, Charles," Andrea snapped. "That isn't even my sexual orientation."

Charles glanced at her face, surprised.

"Another area in which I strive to remain opaque."

"But eventually what Underwood was doing became public."

"Yes, he approached too many women, and eventually the department found out. Enough people knew I was involved that I couldn't cover it up. The department was actually rather kind, they chose not to expel me for the plagiarism and wrote me a rather nice letter of recommendation for Berkeley."

"But you didn't stay there."

"No. I guess what we'd call today post traumatic stress made me restless. I left at the end of the year, took the next year off, and then eventually made my way to the University of Chicago, where I stayed to get my degree. Like you I had preferred my middle name, but while there, I started using my real first name to throw people off the scent. Then I got the job here and everything was rosy."

"Until Underwood showed up."

"And called me immediately to say that things were going right back to the way they were. And if I didn't like it, he would tell the department about my history of plagiarism. It might not get me fired right away, but it would probably prevent my getting tenure. I went to see him that day, to plead with him to not do this again. But he just laughed at me and turned his back. That's when I picked up the trophy and hit him over the head. I knew right away that he was dead."

"And you went back to your office. And you saw Greg go into my office?"

"Yes, and come out again without raising the alarm. So I just waited a few minutes and followed him out."

"And saw me in the parking lot and encouraged me to have it out with Underwood. You tried to put me in the frame."

"I didn't think you'd be in trouble for long. I figured you'd quickly be cleared. But at least it would confuse things enough that I wouldn't be an obvious suspect."

"Why did you kill Sylvia Underwood?"

"I happened to see her on campus the day after her husband died. I could tell she half recognized me. She's been with her husband at

Yale, and we'd met. I figured it was only a matter of time before she'd remember my name and go to the police. I had no choice."

"And Deborah Gould?"

"She also recognized me from Yale. I was Underwood's graduate assistant for her course. I asked her not to tell anyone that I'd been there because it was embarrassing to me. She promised, but had second thoughts once the killing started. I could tell she was ready to cave and talk either to you or the police."

"And you had no choice but to kill me either."

"The first time, on your patio, I was just trying to misdirect the police into thinking you were the intended victim. The rat in the car was meant to scare you off the case. Finally I had no choice but to shoot to kill. I tried to get you to leave things along, but you can be persistent."

"You missed. Did you have second thoughts?" Charles asked hopefully.

She shook her head. "Your friend moved at just the wrong time, too bad for her. We Texas girls usually hit what we aim at. You may not believe me, but I'm glad she didn't die."

"So you would actually have killed me. I thought . . ."

"That I loved you?

"Well, you were always around the house when Barbara was alive. I thought I was your friend."

"Barbara was my friend, and more than that."

Charles felt a hand squeeze his heart. "What do you mean?"

"I didn't come around to see both of you. I came around for Barbara. We were lovers. Surely your didn't think the little bit of affection you had left over after a day with the books was enough for her. We loved each other with a passion. And just so you won't go to your death with any mysteries, the reason Barbara was on the road so late that night is that we were together. We'd met right after work and gone back to a little apartment we rented in Burlington. I asked her not to leave that night in that terrible snowstorm, but she insisted that she had to get back to you. So in a way, her death is all your fault."

Charles shook his head stubbornly. "I don't believe you. She loved me."

"She loved Amy and she loved me. I think for you, Charles, she felt only a sense of responsibility. The kind of responsibility you might feel for someone you once loved."

Charles didn't move, his head hanging low.

"Are you going to shoot me now?" he finally asked.

"No, we'll go into your office, and we'll make it look like a suicide. That will be quite believable. After all, you've just lost your job of forty-years, your girlfriend's been shot, and your last words to your daughter could reasonably be interpreted as a sign of despair. We both know that you have an even better reason now to want it all to be over."

She ordered Charles to stand up. Slowly he did so, and she marched him out of her office and down the hall to his own. Although Charles looked around, hopeful that someone might come down the hall, it didn't happen. She carefully closed the office door behind him.

"Now you're going to sit at your desk and write your last piece of prose: an eloquent suicide note."

"It will never work. Someone will figure it out."

"Lieutenant Thorndike, maybe. I like my chances, Charles."

Her voice was calm now, secure with a sense of victory. Her plans were about to be complete. Somewhere beneath the numbness and despair, Charles found a small hard core of resistance. He was ready to refuse to write the note. To demand that she shoot him without a note and thus leave open the possibility of his death being see as another murder. But suddenly a thought occurred to him. It was a chance—a slender one—but yet a chance.

"You put that rat in my car, knowing that it was one of my greatest fears."

"Sorry, Charles, you had to be stopped. I tried to stop you without it coming to this."

"I understand. I have to go in my desk to get a pen and paper."

She nodded.

Charles slid open the center drawer of his desk and glanced down to see that the rubber snake was still there. He picked it up with his right hand and half-rising flung it forcefully in the direction of Andrea.

Fortunately it was very realistic and in the shadowy office appeared to be the real thing. Her phobia took control. She gave a

206

high-pitched scream and leapt backward. By then Charles had come around the desk, and by the time Andrea began to recognize that the snake was not real, Charles had seized the hand with the gun. She fired, sending a shot through the ceiling of the office. Then she began to twist her wrist, hoping to angle the barrel at Charles head. He reached back with his right arm and hit her in the jaw with a short, hard punch. Her eyes rolled back in her head, and the gun fell from her hand.

He had just picked the gun up from the floor when the door opened and the Lieutenant charged inside. In a second she took in the scene.

"Good work, Charles," she said, taking a pair of cuffs off her belt. "Looks like your daughter needn't have been worried when she called me, you took care of things yourself."

The door opened again and Ernest Ritter stood there looking enraged.

"Someone fired a bullet through the floor of my office." He saw the gun in Charles' hand. "Arrest that man," he said to the Lieutenant, "he tried to kill me."

Charles pointed the gun in the little man's general direction.

"It's been a hard day, Ritter, don't tempt me."

Chapter Forty

Charles was back in the police station. Five days had passed
since Andrea was arrested for the murder of Underwood, his wife
and Deborah Goould. He had called Amy and given her a brief
rundown on what had happened. She had been shocked and
saddened by the idea of Andrea being a murderer. Although Charles
hadn't mentioned anything about Barbara's relationship with
Andrea, he felt that on some level Amy would have been less
shocked than he had been. Perhaps she had sensed that the
relationship between the two of them was not that of a surrogate
mother and daughter. That might have been behind her dislike of
Andrea. He had been oblivious to so much in his own home with his
closest family. She must have been aware of more than he.

He was in the police station to give his account of what had
happened between himself and Andrea that day. A smiling young
woman who appeared to be a civilian had given him a clean white
pad and a pen and asked him to write. Although the arthritis in his
fingers bothered him a bit as he wrote his story out in long hand, he
found that an account of the day flowed easily and naturally.
However this account, too, left out the revelation about Barbara.
Charles felt safe doing this because somehow he doubted that
Andrea would mention it. When he was done and the girl had taken
away his composition, he was told to wait, and that the Lieutenant
would see him soon.

He had been out running each of the five days since the arrest,
the last two accompanied by Greg. The exercise helped clear his
mind and filled him with at least temporary optimism. He had spent
much of his non-running time trying to absorb the events of the past
few days, especially what he had learned about Andrea and Barbara.
Each morning as he awakened the shock seemed a shade less. He
found that, although on a superficial level he had been surprised by
Barbara's relationship with Andrea, on a deeper level it served to
confirm a feeling he'd had for several years before her death that she
was slipping away from him. At the time he'd only half thought
about it, being focused more on his work. And when her

preoccupation with other things did come to the center of his attention, he had easily dismissed it as being due to Barbara's interest in her work. So they had drifted into a late middle-aged routine of two people living separate but parallel lives. He had assumed she'd been as satisfied with this life as he had been. Now he knew that he had been wrong. She had wanted more from life, and had found it. Perhaps he should have wanted more as well.

Now he did, with urgency that he hadn't felt since he was a young man anxious to make his mark. He had accomplished what he could as a scholar. Now was the time to take up a new way of life. What would he do? He knew that the answer to that question wouldn't come all at once. He would keep running, working in the soup kitchen, and stay on the alert for new opportunities to expand the horizons of his life. One thing was certain, he had spent a lifetime trying to understand the life and thought of others, now was the time to begin understanding himself.

Lieutenant Thorndike entered the room and took the chair across from Charles. She smiled with a mixture of joy and relief.

"Thanks for coming in and giving your statement. Everything you said corresponds with the statement Andrea has given to us. She made a complete confession to everything."

"The three murders."

"And the three—actually four—attempts on your life."

"She had a good reason for killing Underwood. He was a monster."

"Yes, a jury would have been sympathetic to that, but it's harder to justify killing Sylvia and Deborah. That was just ruthlessly tying up loose ends. I'm afraid it's going to be a long time, if ever, before Andrea gets out of prison."

Charles nodded somberly. "I'm sorry to hear that because I thought of her as a friend. But I can understand how justice would require it."

"Well, let's get you out of here and back to normal life," Thorndike said cheerfully.

They exited the room and headed up the hall to the entrance to the police station. Suddenly, Charles had an idea on how to expand his horizons. He didn't even think before speaking because he knew that thought could be the enemy of action.

"Lieutenant, if I'm not even a marginal suspect anymore, would you like to go out to dinner with me sometime. I know I may seem a bit dull. I'm not a man of action like most of the men you know."

"I spend my day surrounded by men who act without thinking. In my off hours I prefer to spend my time with a man who thinks more than he acts. Of course, I'll go to dinner with you. When?"

"Tomorrow."

"That would be nice. One thing though."

"What's that?"

"You've got to stop calling me Lieutenant, unless you're really getting off on the uniform."

"What should I call you?"

"The men I work with call me Thorndike, but it would be nice to hear a man call me Joanna."

"Joanna it is, then," Charles said cheerfully. The he recalled how he had gotten off on the wrong foot with Karen by not asking enough about her past.

"Did you go to college?"

She eyed him suspiciously. "Why? Is that a requirement for going out with me?"

"Not at all. I just wanted to know more about you, and that's the kind of thing we former college teachers ask."

She thought about that for a moment, and then nodded.

"Where did you go?"

"Westfield State."

"Did you major in criminal justice?"

"No, philosophy. I originally intended to go to law school."

"What changed your mind?"

"I decided I wanted to pend my life helping people, not reading dry books." Suddenly she appeared stricken. "Sorry, I didn't mean to offend you."

"Not at all," Charles said. "Actually I'm coming around to that way of thinking myself."

Thank you for purchasing this book. If you enjoyed A BODY IN MY OFFICE, you may also like the second book in the series, DEATH OF A SURVIVALIST, and the third, TO DIE FOR ART. For an overview of all my books, please go to glenebisch.com. If you wish to be on my newsletter list, leave your name and email address on my contacts page at my website, and I will add you to my list.

As always, if you enjoyed a book, a review on amazon would be appreciated.

Printed in Great Britain
by Amazon

77173308R00122